R

Innsmouth

by

HENRY HINDER

To Matthew Burke
(who co-created these characters, I guess)
(although I think we both know who did most of the leg-work)
(hint: not you)

And to Ellyse
(my lovely fiancée)

Chapter One.

Before we begin, I believe it would be appropriate to tell you why I am writing this story at all. My reasoning is thus: I am writing this account as a matter of record, and an urgent one at that, as every time I think back to the events that you will soon read over, I am certain a few of the details immeasurably shift and are forever lost. I therefore believe it to be of the utmost importance that I set this affair down in stone before the story becomes only a faint shadow of what truly happened that unexplainable night.

Now, then. Let us begin.

***

I suppose it's only fitting that strange ends come from strange beginnings, and so it was with how I first came into the acquaintance of the peculiar creature I now call my dear friend Bill.

I have always had strange and vivid dreams, ever since I was a boy. Dreams that seemed less like the wild imaginings of my own mind and more like astral journeys into a separate reality that resides in a time and place far distant from our own. The fantastical locations I visited at nights, and the wondrous characters I met, remained perfectly consistent between dreams, and I soon came to know my sleeping world nearly as well as my waking one. Of course, the locations were not always fantastical, and the characters not always wondrous – in fact, both were very often terrifying and nightmarish – but, on the whole, I can say I enjoyed my slumbering voyages.

In my teenage years, I began to search for a meaning to these unusual dreams, as by then it had become abundantly clear to me that my nights were not like those of others. I trawled through internet forums for signs that I was not alone in my experiences, and sure enough found a community of people alluding to visiting a world that sounded unexplainably similar to my own. They too had descended the Seventy Steps of Lighter Slumber and found the Cavern of Flame. They too had walked through the cat-infested streets of Ulthar and heard the distant whisperings of Kadath. They too had spoken with Atal and seen the phosphorescent fungi that so magically lit the Enchanted Woods where the Zoogs and their kin dwelled. To say this realization shook me to my core would be an understatement. I quickly abandoned the forum and decided it best to push the whole affair out of my mind lest I turn into one of those tinfoil-hat wearing loons. I knew how easy it was to fall down rabbit holes on the internet and so opted for a strategy of complete avoidance on the matter.

As I grew older, my dreams became ever more ordinary, and by the time I was 25, I was lucky to journey to my old familiar dream world more than once every few months. One trip there, however, last October on a particularly cruel night, was so vividly peculiar, so intriguingly distinctive, that despite my best efforts, I could do nothing but follow its insane suggestions and pick back up the torch of occult exploration.

I had descended the Seventy Steps of Lighter Slumber that shone golden in the ethereal light, and passed through the Cavern of Flame, acknowledging Nasht and Kaman-Thah with a nod of the head, before passing through the Sacred Pillar of Fire and descending the Seven Hundred Steps of Deeper Slumber. Emerging in the Enchanted Woods, I made haste to Ulthar – one of my favourite Dreamland towns. So far, nothing had been out of the ordinary and all was as it always had been, but as I petted the hordes of cats that swarmed me on entrance to Ulthar, I heard a growling whisper from a neighboring alley.

"Todd Wyson?"

A chill instantly ran down my spine and my mind began racing with the terrifying implications. Who was beckoning me and how did they know my name? I had only told a few people in the Dreamlands my real name, and I recalled none sounding like the voice I had just heard.

"Todd Wyson?" the grave voice repeated. "Do not be scared. Come here."

With a bravery I did not know I possessed, I made my way towards the alley and my potential doom. Turning the corner, I came face to face with a sight at first monstrous. A figure towered over me, vaguely humanoid in its stance but with the mottled fur and distorted face of something canine in nature. I instantly fell onto my rear and began to scuttle back, but the figure reached out a hand and smiled – it was a smile just human enough to put me at ease. "You have no need to fear me, Todd. I am a friend."

Again, summoning a courage previously unknown to me, I took the cold and unexpectedly rubbery hand of the cryptic creature and got back on my feet with their help. "How do you know my name?" I asked.

"I know many things," they smiled, and I tried not to recoil on seeing up close its rows of jagged fangs. "Now, there is little time to waste so let me tell you quickly what you need to know. My name is Richard Pickman and I am on your side." He paused as he studied my face with curious eyes. "And by *your* side, I mean humanity's. Despite my appearance, I used to be one of you. The details can wait for later – all I need from you now is your trust. So, do you trust me, Todd Wyson? Do I have your trust?"

Through shallow breaths, I forced out a "Yes?" even though the question was not yet decided in my mind. I wished to hear more, however, and decided that would be best accomplished by not aggravating Mr. Pickman.

"Good," he said. "Then drink this." He turned around, crouched his spindly, sparsely-furred legs, and came back up with a gourd full of some apparent liquid. "This will show you what you need to know. I am not privy to the details but I would not ask anything of you if I did not think it of the utmost importance to humanity's survival."

He held out the gourd and I tentatively grasped it. It was far heavier than I was expecting and as I brought the gourd towards myself, I swear I felt the liquid inside swell and surge of its own accord. "What is it?" I asked.

"That, I cannot say. Again, you will simply have to trust me. Now, drink – before we are discovered." At that moment, Pickman looked to the skies with fearful eyes, and looking up too, I noticed the waning crescent moon emanating a sinister quality that I never before knew it had the potential to. He snapped his snout back down and growled, "Quickly."

At his command, I drank. The liquid was queerly bitter and sweet at the same time, and as the substance trickled down my throat, I again thought I felt it undulate spontaneously which nearly made me retch. Before I brought the gourd down from my first sip, I found my surroundings dissolving into an abyssal darkness which stretched out into an endless void. "Good luck," I thought I heard my companion whisper before I was suddenly alone.

"Jackie!" a voice screamed out in the darkness. "Jackie! No!" The voice was hoarse and wrapped in what I inferred to be an extremely thick Australian accent. Looking down, I found my legs had decided to move towards the screams of their own accord, and soon, out of the darkness, emerged a most disturbing and sinister vision.

A man in a thick, leather overcoat was being held, arms behind back, by an oily, jet-black, horned creature that barely stood out against the inky darkness. As I still further approached, drawn towards the distressing scene by a form of psychic magnetism, I noticed the slick and evil creature bore a pair of fleshy wings too. The man cried out again as he stared into the void, desperately seeking to break free of the devil's grasp. "Jackie!" the man sobbed, breaking down in tears. "Oh, Jackie…"

And then the creature took flight with a silent beat of its wings, and ascended into the shadowed heavens with the wretched man still in its hold. And just like that, I was once again left alone in utter blackness.

"Bill," a voice came to me on whispered winds. "His name is Bill. You must seek him."

The next thing I remember was waking up in my dingy New York apartment drenched in hot sweat, even though the night outside was veritably freezing. I sat up and tried to process all I had just experienced. Failing that, I got out of bed, poured myself a stiff drink and stared out the window at the twinkling city skyline. The moon was full and had lost all its ominous qualities – in fact, I recall it looking rather friendly as moons go. After finishing my drink, and then another, I decided it would probably be wise to return to sleep, but as I turned away from the window

I just so happened to notice the peculiar way the moonlight was falling through the gap in the curtains. It was forming a pillar of silver light, perfectly pointing to and illuminating my laptop on the floor. To me, it was a clear sign. Filled with a curiosity and an eagerness I had not yet felt since childhood, I sprung to my laptop and immediately opened a portal to the worldwide web.

I searched for the Bill I had seen in that vision all through the rest of the night – on my old forums, on Facebook, on Twitter. My efforts proved fruitless. By daybreak, I was exhausted and resigned myself to sleep again, thoroughly dejected. I dreamt only of my old job cycling around the city as a Deliveroo rider. The sad reality was Deliveroo had recently parted ways with me for, on occasion, eating the customers' food before delivery. In my defense, however, I was not paid nearly well enough to afford food for myself as well as rent.

Several days later, by which time I had lost all hope that my dream had been anything more than a feverish hallucination, I was on an explicit site (which I shall not give free advertising to until they refund me for my 'free' trial) when an advert by the side of the video player caught my eye. It seemed to be a close-up picture of the man I had seen in my drunken vision – Bill – performing a double thumbs up with an expansive grin spread across his face. The portrait bordered on a picture of insanity, and I secretly prayed to whatever gods might be listening that this was not the man I should be seeking. All doubt of his identity was readily resolved, however, when I read the plain text underneath, 'Bill: The Cosmic Entity Control Expert For All Your Cosmic Needs!'

I pulled up my pants, clicked on the ad, and within seconds found myself on a most dated and confusing website. Popups informed me in multicolored text that I could get 50% off my first cosmic extermination, or a free *My First Necronomicon (Perfect for Kids!)* on all orders over $3000. With much difficulty, I navigated to the 'About Me' page.

Hey there, buddy! Thanks for visiting my internet page. The name's Bill. How ya bloody doing?

I've been a professional Cosmic Entity Control Expert for over thirty years. My dad was one before me so I guess you could say I followed in his footsteps — he went missing when I was pretty young though, so I had to imagine a lot of the footsteps! HA!

I know cosmic shit can get pretty confusing pretty fast, so that's exactly why if you're ever in any doubt, you shouldn't hesitate to hire someone like me, an expert, to come and deal with it for you (for an extremely reasonable price) before you lose your sanity/soul/life. It's just not worth it.

I offer exterminations, negotiations, cult management courses, otherworldly cleaning, minor plumbing, and exorcisms, plus any other unique requests you might want — so just shoot me a fax, why don't ya? I don't bite! Much!

Seriously though, I've worked through that problem and I'm much better now, so I hope to hear from you soon. No task is too big or too small for Old Bill, and don't worry about thinking I won't believe ya — I've been through some pretty insane stuff! And not in the fun colloquial sense but in the very real sense of permanently damaging my mental health. Anyway, see ya!

Now, I had read about occult and esoteric subjects before – when investigating my dreams as a teen – but never before had I met someone who believed in their reality so much as to base their livelihood on it. I did not know precisely what he meant by cosmic entities but presumed it related to the creatures I encountered in my peculiar dreams – either that or he was a fraud of the highest order who spent his life siphoning money away from gullible fools. That is to say, all in all, I didn't know quite what to make of him or his business.

I decided there was only one sensible course of action that lay ahead of me, however. If what Mr. Pickman had told me was true – that humanity's survival somehow depended on my seeking out this Bill – then surely there was nothing left for me to do but pack my bags and meet him for myself.

This course of action also agreed with me for two other reasons. One: I hadn't paid rent in two months and the landlord had informed me that he would like to break my legs for this; and two: I was very lonely.

***

After finding an address on Bill's website, I quickly spent the last of my money on a Greyhound bus ticket to Massachusetts which left later that afternoon. I packed my belongings into one suitcase with a broken strap and went on my way.

The bus journey passed by extremely slowly so I busied myself by studying the remainder of Bill's website. His client appraisals were most perplexing, alluding to strange occurrences that were either totally false or else insinuating the reality of supernatural affairs far outside my realm of knowledge or prior experience.

Here are a few extracts for you to get a better sense of what I mean:

I originally paid for a psychic to come round but her head exploded, so I was very pleased when Bill managed to subdue the "spawn of Nodens" without dying gruesomely in my newly-carpeted living room. 5/5 stars! – Ethyl, Boston

Bill was a great help in imprisoning Nyctelios in the underwater citadel of Atheron, and a fountain of knowledge regarding the history of Elder Gods. He's also just a bloody good bloke, and a laugh and a half! – Theodore, Adelaide

Bill is such an awesome guy. His prices may seem steep but I promise they're worth every cent because he really knows what he's on about and also he's as handsome as all hell. He can do anything and he's really cool and he 100% did not tickle the nipples of the seven triples when commanded to. Also, he's completely not mental. – Smill

Again, I didn't know whether to believe what I was reading or not, and thought it better to reserve all judgement until I had the chance to meet the man for myself.

It was approaching dusk when I reached the address, and the orange hues that filled the sky provided an eerie backdrop for what would have been a haunting sight even in full light. The house exuded a terrible and dark aura hard to put into words. I immediately had the sense that hellish deeds must have occurred inside in centuries past, and that some residue of their evil still lingered. The outside walls were unpainted and dark from decades of neglect, and the roof was unnaturally steep. To the side, an outside flight of stairs led up to the second story, suffocated by a tangle of ivy so dense that my mind could not help but leap to disturbing conclusions on its nutrient-rich food source.

Despite all this, I approached the decaying front door and rang the bell. I waited several minutes before ringing again, and several minutes after that too. I presumed him to be away from the property at present and so went to find a local café or bar to pass the time when I heard a faint source of something akin to music. It was coming from round the side of the house and so, with nothing better to do, I resolved to investigate. I followed the source of the strange, arrhythmic noise until I noticed it was coming from some low windows that seemed to provide light for a lower basement. Approaching the window, I bent down and looked through. Inside, to my delight, I caught my first glimpse of Bill in the flesh. He was stood in front of an easel, a paintbrush in his mouth, and his hands ripping at his graying, wild hair. The canvas was facing away from me and so I could not see what he was working on but it seemed to be causing him much distress. The basement was filled with various old technologies, tomes, equipment, and parchments – most strewn carelessly across the floor.

In the mess, I managed to spot the record player from which the mad, only semi-melodic music was blasting forth. Determined to get his attention, I rapped on the window. Bill instantly snapped his eyes to me with an intensity I was not prepared for. I waved to show my friendly intentions, but this only seemed to anger him further. I pointed towards the front door as I stepped back, hoping for him to understand my meaning, but he merely continued to stand behind his canvas, confused and irate. I made for the front door in any case and rang the doorbell again.

Thirty seconds later, the door swung open and I began my introduction. "Hi, I'm Todd. Todd Wyson. Are you Bi——?"

"——What the fuck d'you think you're doing creeping around my backyard, ya bloody freak?" he spat, his Australian accent just as thick as it was in my dream.

"I, um, I," I sputtered, not rehearsed for such a hostile first interaction. "I've come because… I have something I have to discuss with you."

"Something to discuss with me? Sorry, but who the fuck even are you? If you ain't got business for me, fuck off. Mormon prick." He slammed the door shut, and I stood shocked.

Quickly coming to my senses, I rang the doorbell again and shouted through the letterbox, "I'm not a Mormon! I have something very important to tell you! Something you'll want to hear!" After a moment of hesitation, I heard his footsteps approaching the door again, and he begrudgingly opened it back up.

"What?" he grunted. "Get on with it, then trot off back to whatever sad lonely hole you came from. I've got important shit to be getting on with."

"I saw you in a dream," I said, swallowing. "I was told I needed to seek you out by this... well, this werewolfy-type thing called Richard Pickman. He said it was of the utmost importance to humanity's survival."

Bill furrowed his brow, appearing to seriously consider the validity of my tale. "That's the dumbest shit I've ever heard." He went to slam the door shut again but I grabbed it before it could close.

"Jackie!" I blurted out. "Jackie..." All color drained from his face as he let the door swing back open.

"How d'you know that name?" he said quietly, his skin now as pale as the moon. He then leapt towards me, grabbing my collar and yanking me in tight. "How do you know that name?" he screamed, his eyes as wild as a rabid dog's, spittle flying from his foaming mouth.

"My dream," I screamed back. "I heard you shout it in my dream. Why? Does it mean something to you?"

His face contorted in a pained grimace, and he began shaking, before completely dropping the act, letting me go, and stepping back with a smug grin on his face. "Nah, mate. I'm fucking with you. Just thought it'd be funny." I was now extremely bewildered, and could only manage to sputter a few noises that sounded vaguely questioning. "You seriously thought saying a name you heard in a dream would mean anything at all to me? You thought some random sheila's name would change my mind and welcome you in with open arms? Where d'you grow up?" Bill seemed to search for an appropriate answer. "…Fairytale land?"

"So, you don't believe me?" I asked.

Bill sniffed and wiped his nose, looking away. "I didn't say that." He turned into his house and, clearly with much reluctance, mumbled, "Come in. It's about to rain."

The sky was as clear as an unmuddied lake.

***

"And you weren't told nothing 'bout *why* you had to come to me?" Bill said as he handed me a mug of boiling water. "Out of teabags," he explained.

"No, nothing." I said, taking a sip of my modest drink.

"I think I might know why," he replied before letting loose a crafty smile. "I've been looking for a new assistant."

"Oh, really?" I said.

"Yep. Naturally, the position would be unpaid at first – for a year or two – you know, just to see if we're a good fit or not, but I could offer free lodging in the spare bedroom upstairs. If ya can fix the bed."

"Right," I said, the whole proposition being rather a lot to take in at a moment's notice.

"So, we'll start tomorrow?" he replied, moving towards me and taking away the mug of hot water I had hardly drunk.

"Um," I began. "Well... You said free lodging?"

"Sure, sure," he said. "But you'll have to work for your stay." He left the room for the kitchen, and shouted behind him, "Your room's the first on the left at the top of the stairs. Make yourself at home-slash-work. Got some paperwork I wouldn't mind some help with tonight, actually."

Before I had a chance to find my bearings in this new life I had somehow inadvertently stepped into, a stack of tax forms were in my arms and I was being pushed up the stairs by a now exorbitant Bill. "Dunno what this has gotta do with humanity's survival, but I'm sure glad you came along now – I've got so much for you to do."

Despite my admittedly meagre protests, Bill would not take no for an answer, and I soon found myself working through his papers at my new rickety desk. This was to be the first night of many spent as Bill's assistant/butler/accountant/ housemate.

In fact, it is at that very same desk that I am now writing this book.

Chapter Two.

Waking up in my new and wonky bed, which had more broken springs in it than working ones, I found Bill standing over me, eyes wide open.

"I hope you don't mind, mate. While you were sleeping, I went through your phone – just to check you out, you know? Make sure you're not mental. Get some references."

"What?" I said, startled fully into the world of the waking. "Who did you message?"

"Well, that's the thing," he said. "You didn't have no-one in it. Other than your landlord. Don't you have no friends?"

"Did you… ask my landlord about me?"

"Yeah," he said. "Called him. He wanted to know where you were. Sounded very angry."

"And did you tell him?"

"Yeah, course."

I jumped out of bed and began hurriedly collecting my clothes. "I'm afraid I'm going to have to leave." I stuffed a pair of socks in my pocket. "Thank you very much for your hospitality but that man is a maniac. He has it out for me. I'm not safe here."

Bill laughed. "I told him where you were – didn't say I told him the truth. Said you'd gone to live in North Alaska. Said you'd become a fisherman."

I stopped and studied Bill's face. It appeared he was telling the truth. I sighed and felt my whole body relax. "Oh, thank god."

"Don't thank him. Thank me – maybe with a nice fried brekkie?" He then smiled at me with eyes that would have put any puppy to shame, and I found I could do nothing but oblige.

***

Gradually, I began to settle into my new role and accommodate myself within my unfamiliar surroundings. Bill was not difficult to live with per se, but rather idiosyncratic in his ways, and it took a little while before I was something close to comfortable in his presence. He had a penchant for gargling at random times, and seemed to make a hobby of mumbling a strange language to himself whilst staring vacantly at certain paintings or statuettes. I often wondered what was going through his peculiar mind at such times.

He was also extremely particular about what objects I could or could not touch around the house. For instance, one possession he was exceptionally protective of was a revolver I found in a drawer one morning during a snooping expedition designed to relieve my acute boredom and intense curiosity as to Bill's true nature.

As I picked up the rusty, engraved, long-barreled firearm, Bill suddenly materialized, as if from the ether, and snatched it from my hands. "Don't you dare bloody touch that," he snapped. "This is me dad's revolver – he left it for me." He looked at the gun lovingly, and stroked it tenderly. "Or he just left it," he added with a shrug. "Didn't say." He placed the revolver carefully back in the drawer before shoving an extended finger in my face. "Be careful touching shit round here," he said portentously. "Half of it'll kill ya…" He lingered, staring into my eyes, unblinking. "The other half… I dunno, just don't touch it."

"Alright," I swallowed, and that seemed enough to satisfy him as he quickly stormed off to get back to whatever had been occupying him previously.

There were other peculiarities about Bill too that kept my mind wondering. I had no clue as to when he slept back then, as often throughout the night I could hear him going about some business; playing music; tinkering with equipment; or reading out loud to himself. And when I say out loud, I do mean loud. I could only half understand the books he read, so full of occult and esoteric jargon as they were, but what I heard intrigued me to no end. I felt my old curiosities returning – the ones that had kept me up nights and nights on end trawling through forums.

Furthermore, the music he listened to or played on his violin was like nothing I had ever heard before.

He only seemed to practice his music when up in his room in the loft, and only around the hours of midnight, and as such, it often kept me awake as the sounds that recurrently came from that diabolic instrument seemed diametrically opposed to the idea of sleep, such violent and horrific imagery did they inspire.

After a couple of weeks or so, I was into a steady daily routine of various activities which I will outline here:

8:00am – Run Bill a hot bath and set a timer for two hours so he can enter once cooled.

8:10am – Go to the shops and buy Bill a loaf of fresh bread, a dozen eggs, a pack of smokey bacon, and six sausages.

8:30am – Cook Bill his breakfast.

9:00am – Wash the dishes.

9:15am – Cook Bill another breakfast.

9:25am – Wash the dishes.

9:30am – Do the laundry.

10:00am – Tell Bill his bath is cool now.

10:15am – Have my assigned one slice of toast for breakfast.

01:00pm – Remind Bill to get out of bath.

01:30pm – Remind Bill to get out of bath.

02:00pm – Remind Bill to get out of bath.

02:30pm – Pour a bowl of mixed nuts for Bill's lunch.

03:00pm – Watch Bill tinker with equipment in the basement (if I've been good).

03:30pm – Dust the entire house.

06:00pm – Have my assigned one slice of toast for lunch.

06:30pm – Try to teach Bill how to order takeout pizza again, then just order it for him instead.

07:30pm – Collect pizza, place each slice on a different plate, then bring them all through to Bill.

08:00pm – Enjoy Bill's crusts.

08:30pm – Watch an episode of The Crocodile Hunter on VHS with Bill.

09:30pm – Make Bill his bedtime sandwich.

10:00pm – Do any paperwork that needs doing.

10:30pm – Make Bill another bedtime sandwich.

11:00pm – Try to sleep.

12:00pm – Get woken up by Bill's insane violin playing.

Of course, this routine was often broken by spontaneous requests and unique interruptions, such as Bill coming to me one morning whilst I was attending to the laundry and informing me that it was time to begin my training proper. This excited me to no end, and I found my palms clamming up in anticipation as he drew me into his study and sat me down for my first lesson on cosmic entities.

"Right," he began. "How much do you know about cosmic creatures and old gods and all that?"

"Not much," I said. "I mean, I've heard of Cthulhu."

Bill groaned and rolled his eyes. "Everyone's heard of fucking Cthulhu. That's like me asking if you know about music and you saying you've heard of The

Beatles. I'm just gonna assume you know jack shit then, alright?"

"That's probably best," I admitted.

Bill took a pen and tapped a strangely elongated skull beside him. "I'm just gonna start going and I'm not gonna stop so if you have any questions, don't ask them, 'cos I don't want you to mess up my flow or anything, so, right, here we go. The beings I deal with are like nothing else on Earth or anything you've ever encountered before. In fact, most of them are from different dimensions. The longer you work with me, the more you'll realize that ordinary life is just a thin shell over a reality so alien and abstract in comparison, and filled with such incomprehensible horrors that merely contemplating them should turn anyone in their right mind insane." Bill then gargled loudly for around five seconds before leaping to his feet and frantically drawing out a family tree on a chalkboard pulled out from the side of his cobweb-infested bookcase.

After finishing the diagram, he proudly presented it to me. "There are lots of different types of cosmic entities," he began, slapping the bottom of the board. "At your most basic, you've got your servant races like your Formless Spawn or your Rat-Things." His hand shifted up the tree. "Further up, you've got your lesser gods like Daoloth, The Render of the Veils; Nyctelios, big loser; Tsathugghua, Sleeper of N'kai; Shudde M'Ell, The Burrower Beneath; and *yes*, Cthulhu." He groaned again before moving his attention to the top of the board. "And up here you've got your great elder gods like Azathoth, The Blind Idiot God who's colossal dream we are all in; Yog-Sothoth, The Lurker at the Threshold; Yog-Hypnos, The Unholy Lord of Nightmares; Yog-Nogon, if you're dealing with cosmic terror then he's probably had his tentacles in it; and finally we've got the great Yog-Urt!" Bill snatched up his old pot of yogurt from the desk and laughed to himself hysterically. "Nah, nah, only kidding," he managed to push out between wheezes. "Well, it is yogurt, it's just not a god." He took a mouthful which, from the expression on his face, seemed at odds with his taste buds. "You know what I mean."

"Right," I said, having not really understood any of what I had just been told. "So, what has any of this got to do with my dreams?"

"Well," Bill began, scraping the leftover yogurt off his tongue. "That Dreamland you go to is one manifestation of this perpendicular dimension our world resides on and from which these creatures come. Obviously there's some soothsayer there who's seen some terrible portent of the future and thinks for some reason that putting us two together might be able to stop it." Bill shrugged. "That's my reading of the situation, but, I dunno, maybe that's all bollocks. Maybe you're just some hallucinating freak and maybe I'm just an old fool. Only thing to do is wait and see."

***

In the first month or so I spent in Bill's company, it appeared to me that he had not once received a job of any sort – and the tax report I had filled out for him on my first night seemed to indicate that business was the very opposite of booming. Some days I felt sorry for the old man, but on others, those on which I was feeling more cynical (such as one morning after having spent three and a half hours scrubbing away at a particularly stubborn and mysterious stain on his vest), I found myself wondering whether perhaps his 'work' was nothing more than a figment of his mad imagination. Whether perhaps this world of gods and cosmic entities he had built up around him was all a self-serving delusion – a case of daydreams taken too seriously. A way for the lonely fool to feel purpose in this purposeless world.

In want of getting a little closer to the truth of the matter, I confronted him with my observation one night whilst making him his obligatorily-crustless sandwich to see how he'd react. At my remark, he sighed a weary sigh. "I can't lie to ya, mate. You're right. Business has dried up." He pulled out a chair and slumped into it as I handed him his first bedtime snack. "People just ain't as open to the supernatural anymore," he said, taking a huge bite of the sandwich and struggling to swallow it. "They just explain it away now with… science and denial and shit. But it's still out there! The unexplainable. The incomprehensible. The indescribable. It's still out there, and in our neglect, it's getting stronger…" Bill seemed to stare through me, as if caught in a timeless void, as if seeing something only those who have known true terror could see. "Bubble's gonna burst,

Todd. Soon enough, bubble's gonna burst. Then we'll be laughing!" Bill threw back his head in a laughter so psychotic, so deranged and manic, that the answer to my question seemed as plain as day. Was he insane or was everything he saying really true? His gaping spasming mouth told me all I needed to know. Bill was mental – that was all there was to it. Totally, utterly mental.

I resolved to leave the house the next day.

***

I was lying in bed when I heard Bill begin his nightly violin practice. I almost immediately noticed something different about it that time though – a sort of desperation that leaked into the chaotic babel of notes that wasn't usually there. It wasn't that the sound was hideous, for it was not; but that it held vibrations suggesting nothing else I had heard before, and assumed a certain symphonic quality which I could scarcely believe was coming from one instrument.

As I rose to my feet, determined to witness Bill's playing with my own eyes for the first time, and possibly the last, the playing quickly began to swell, and become, somehow, even more frenzied and otherworldly. I quickly made haste out of my room and up the stairs to the loft, where I found the door locked as Bill's music reached a pandemonium that would have led me to doubt my own shaking sanity had I not looked through the keyhole and seen for myself Bill's crazed bowing and terrified expression. It would be useless to try and describe the height of insanity Bill's playing reached as I tried desperately to break through the door, as candles spluttered around the room. As Bill played, his gaze never strayed from the window, an expression of stark fear affixed to his face as the curtains fluttered with an almost malign intent in the nighttime wind. It seemed to me that he was in a battle, though with what, I could not imagine. Then, from the window, I half fancied I heard an exquisitely low and infinitely distant musical note.

This seemed to push Bill over the edge into the depths of hysteria and made his playing less musical than I ever thought an instrument could sound. As I stared through the keyhole, desperately trying to barge the door open, I could almost see shadowy satyrs and bacchanals dancing and whirling insanely through seething abysses of clouds and smoke and lightning. It was then that I thought I heard that distant note from the window grow shriller, more deliberate, more purposeful, and take on shades of a sinister mocking.

Finally, the door gave way, splintering at the frame, and I burst into the dim-lit room, though Bill was too absorbed to pay me any notice. I rushed to his side, and looked out through the window that he was so transfixed by. I looked out expecting to see the trees and fellow houses of Massachusetts but saw nothing of the sort; only the blackness of space illimitable; unimagined space alive with motion and music, and having no semblance of anything on earth. And as I stood there, looking in terror, the wind blew out all the candles surrounding us, leaving me in a savage and impenetrable darkness with chaos and pandemonium my only footholds on sanity.

Before I passed out from sheer hysteria, and from what I could make out in the darkness, with a final flick of his bow, Bill somehow generated a force or sound or spell strong enough to slam the window shut, and whip close its curtains. Seconds later, with the flick of a match, Bill lit the room again and went around relighting the candles. I stared at him in wonder and amazement. What had I just witnessed? What powers did he truly possess? What horror was he dueling with?

With a stretch of his arms, Bill yawned and coolly announced, "Alright, me sleepy now. Time for beddy-byes." He then strode out of the loft, violin in hand, as if nothing more than a simple chess match had occurred. "You're paying for the door, by the way," he yelled out as he descended the stairs. I stayed behind and collected my thoughts, as scattered as they were.

It seemed as if I had been previously mistaken in the conclusion to my question of whether Bill was insane or whether all he had told me was true. After what I had just witnessed, it slowly dawned on me that the question had been somewhat of a false dichotomy; for now I realized that it was totally possible, and in fact, infinitely likely, that Bill was not just utterly insane, but *also* a teller of truth. And, in fact, the two were inextricably linked.

Chapter Three.

About two months into my residence with Bill, I was granted another voyage to the Dreamlands. As always, I went through the motions of descending both the steps of Lighter and Deeper Slumber, and began to traverse through the twilight-glowing Enchanted Woods. I hoped to make the acquaintance of Mr. Pickman again in Ulthar to relay what had occurred since last we met, and to enquire as to just what was the purpose of my newfound servitude to the strange and stern Bill. Before I could leave the Enchanted Woods, however, I felt a sharp pain shoot up my right leg. I looked down and saw my foot in the middle of a most intricately designed circular rune aglow with a magical, golden fire that burnt cleanly with no trace of smoke.

Before I could come to any conclusions about what was occurring, I felt my leg pulled down into the middle of the rune, seemingly into the ground that now held no more resistance than air. Within less than a second, the entirety of my body had been pulled beneath the ground and I then proceeded to fall through a vacuum of nothingness. To my surprise, I was not particularly fearful as I fell through limitless time and space, perhaps because of all Bill had taught of the true nature of this place – though most of what he had told me was detailing how dangerous and sanity-destroying it could be. Nonetheless, I soon found myself falling softly out of the void and onto a balcony in the most breathtaking city I have still ever had the pleasure to lay my eyes on.

All golden and lovely it blazed in the sunset, with walls, temples, colonnades and arched bridges of veined marble, silver-basined fountains of prismatic spray in broad squares and perfumed gardens, and wide streets marching between delicate trees and blossom-laden urns and ivory statues in gleaming rows. On steep northward slopes, there climbed tiers of red roofs and old peaked gables harboring little lanes of grassy cobbles. Mystery and wonder hung about the place as clouds about a fabulous unvisited mountain, and as I stood there breathless, on that marble balcony, a familiar voice growled behind me.

"Lovely, isn't it?" Pickman said as he strode out through the French doors to join me. "At least, for now. Sorry about the rough journey, but this was the only way to get you here without prying eyes." Behind him I noticed the fleeting silhouette of a black cat skulking across the room.

"Don't mention it," I said. "I've had worse." My mind instantly jumped back to the Greyhound bus I had taken not too long previous. "Where are we?"

"Somewhere safe," he replied, expertly avoiding the question as the cat poked its head around the corner of the door to inspect the new visitor. Its eyes were a blazing yellow and seemed to suggest an intelligence far beyond your typical feline. "Somewhere we can plan for the things to come," Pickman continued. "First, let me get you a drink." He gestured to the corner of the balcony and before my eyes an onyx globe materialized. "What do you like?"

Astonished, I replied, "Well, what have you got?"

"Anything." He opened the top of the dark planet revealing a mirage of bottles shifting in and out of existence, morphing shapes and colors. "This is a dream, after all."

"Whiskey?"

He smiled at my choice. "One dream whiskey for the gentleman." As he poured my drink into a tumbler that could not decide on what pattern it wished to decorate itself with, I resolved to probe what he had mentioned earlier.

"You said this place was for planning – planning for what is to come. What is that? What is to come?"

Pickman bared his fangs in a strange smile and shook his head as he handed me my whiskey. I took a sip. It was perfect. "I can't tell you that. Chiefly because I'm not entirely sure myself. I'm a pawn just the same as you – albeit a slightly higher one." He then let out something halfway between a laugh and a bark, and that peculiar cat joined in with a portentous meow. "Anyway, what has become of you, Todd Wyson? What did you see in your vision last we met?"

I told him what I saw in that dark and terrible portent, and gave him a truncated account of the previous few months.

"Chores?" he questioned, with a puzzled brow. "You're mostly doing household chores?"

"Well, yeah, mostly," I replied. "I mean, occasionally he teaches me a bit about cosmic beings and old gods and all that, so, I guess, maybe that's why I was sent to him?"

"And you're sure you've got the right Bill?" Pickman rumbled.

"I think so."

"Hmm," he mused, leaning on the gleaming white handrail, and gazing at the wondrous setting sun. He then glanced back to the black cat, which was now sat in the corner slowly and methodically beating its tail on the marble floor. "Perhaps there has been a mistake."

"Really? You think that could happen?"

Pickman shrugged, turning back to me. "Who knows? This is all above our comprehension. The cogs turning are far too colossal for either of us to see. I suppose all there is for you to do is to keep on pulling at this cosmic string – something's bound to happen sooner or later. Oh!" Pickman jolted as if just then remembering something terribly important. He grimaced and laid his rubbery hand on my shoulder. "Happy birthday, Todd."

With these parting words, I was ejected from the dream and back into the squalid interior of my dank bedroom. Checking the date, I found, to my surprise, that yes, it was in fact my 34th birthday. I didn't know quite how to react to this information, and so opted for just running Bill's bath slightly early.

It was a day the same as any other.

In the evening, however, I decided to be a little devious and treat myself to a peek at the painting Bill had been working on in the basement, and which he always kept hidden under a sheet. It had been a mystery on my mind as of late, and I felt finally satisfying my curiosity would do well as a personal birthday gift.

I waited until Bill had retired up to the loft to begin his nightly violin practice (if that word is not too mundane for what I now knew was happening up there), before soundlessly creeping out of my room and descending the two creaky flights of stairs into the basement. There, in the corner, was the covered easel and canvas I sought. I tiptoed towards it, strangely apprehensive about what I was on the verge of uncovering. A portion of my mind felt a twinge of guilt about this arrant invasion of privacy, but thinking back to all Bill had made me do the previous few months seemed to promptly quell these concerns.

Standing in front of the easel, I grasped the sheet, and readied myself for the grand reveal. In one fell motion, I threw the sheet off of the canvas and could not help but shriek in terror at what I saw.

All attempts at describing the grotesqueness of the painting that lay before me are predestined to fail, but I shall try my best to provide some characterization of the incommunicable. In shades of red, dreadfully like that of old blood on parchment, a thousand screaming visages of Bill's own face stared back at me. Every conceivable shade of terror was manifest on that canvas, and, against my will, looking closer, in the very middle of those perturbing portraits I noticed a faint, ebony silhouette. It was the silhouette of a woman — a woman with long flowing hair dancing in ancient winds.

"What d'ya think?" Bill muttered behind me, and I jumped out of my skin for the second time that night.

"It's, uh," I stuttered, "It's... very artistic."

"It's horrible," Bill replied in a markedly somber tone, turning away from the piece and meandering back towards the stairs, brushing his fingers over the myriad leather tomes that lay stacked on top of one another like a city skyline in miniature. "The job's horrible. It's horrible work, Todd. Horrible."

I swallowed, mistrustful of Bill's apparent sincerity, but eager to tease out all I could from him in this abnormal state of candidness. "Then why do you do it?"

"That's a good question," Bill replied. "I mean, end of the day, someone's gotta do it, don't they?" Bill turned around to face me but avoided all eye contact. "And, you know, when me dad went missing, that someone turned out to be me, I guess. Someone's gotta look after these children – and most other men would go mad doing it. But not me," he smiled. "Not me."

He then proceeded to unblinkingly stare at my forehead, whilst not saying a further word, as if trying to drill deep into my mind via the aid of some unknown psychic power. Feeling unsure of what precisely was happening, I took the initiative to turn away and re-drape the sheet over his distressing painting. Looking back, and finding Bill still staring wide-eyed at where I was previously stood, I took the initiative once again to try and continue our dialogue.

"It's actually my birthday today," I said. "I was wondering whether you wanted to have a drink together maybe? To celebrate."

I looked hopefully towards the tired, haggard man that stood before me as he slowly emerged from his stasis. I could almost see him weighing up the proposition in his mind. Unfortunately, his response was less than gratifying – he simply exited the room without a word and went back up to his loft, leaving me feeling more alone and friendless than I had ever yet felt in my new home.

I found myself wondering whether Bill would ever have any inkling of fondness for me, or whether I would simply remain used by him with no more regard than he would show an inanimate tool. Shortly into my wonderings, however, I felt the answer I was heading towards would do my sanity no good, and so dropped the matter.

I went to my room and tried my best to have a happy dream.

***

In the middle of the night, I was awoken by what I thought at first was a terrible earthquake. The reality, however, was far more frightening. Opening my eyes, I found Bill at the foot of my bed, manically shaking my loosely held together bedframe in a frenzy. With a passion I had not heard in his voice before, he announced, "We've got a job, Todd! We've got a fucking job!"

I sat up in bed, surprised at the sudden swell of enthusiasm I could feel rising up within myself. "Really? That's great."

"Yeah! And it's with cults and sacrifices and shit! Proper stuff!"

"Oh," I replied. "Nice?"

"Yeah, that's right! Nice! So, let's get ready and pack the van! Use the list on the board downstairs, and do me a peanut butter and jelly sarnie for the road – no crusts. Be ready for six on the dot, six on the dot!" Bill hurried out of the room, shouting behind him as he scampered down the corridor, "No crusts! No fucking crusts!"

I promptly got to work, and by six, was ready at the front door, van keys in one hand, and sandwich in the other. There was no sign of Bill.

At seven, there was no sign of Bill.

At eight, there was no sign of Bill.

At nine, Bill meandered down the stairs, casually stretching his limbs and yawning carelessly. "What happened? What have you been doing?" I asked incredulously.

"Just fancied a lie in," Bill shrugged. "You got me sarnie?" Without waiting for a response, he ripped the food from my hand and took a big bite. He then pulled a face as if he had just bitten into the most exceptionally sour lemon. "This is gross, Todd. Jesus. How d'you frog up a PBJ sarnie?" Throwing the sandwich in the bin, he yanked the van keys off me, gargled, and strode out of the house. As I stood there in shock and disbelief, he shouted back, "Come on, mate. Hurry up."

***

On the road, after refamiliarizing himself with the shift lever, given it had been over a year since he last drove, Bill finally decided to divulge the details of the job we had received. "So, I was reading some Abdul last night, yeah, when I suddenly heard the fax machine go. Now, you gotta understand, I don't think I've had a fax in, like, four or five years, so this was pretty bloody exciting. You know, it really got me blood going, so I bound on over and ripped the paper out, and this is what it said – more or less. Dear Bill, blah blah blah, living in Innsmouth and there's been some strange shit going on. Me husband has been doin' some investigating 'cos he thinks there's a cult taking old locals and sacrificing them, blah blah blah, one of them was our son, blah blah blah, two nights ago he went out to follow a bunch of weirdos and he hasn't come back. So, can you come and find out what's happened to him? That was basically the gist of it. But, get this, she said she'd be willing to pay us $10,000 just for finding out what happened to the fucksticle – not even saving him! How great is that?"

"Um, yeah, pretty great," I said, my heart uncontrollably quickening – the reality of our having to pry into a likely-sacrificial cult beginning to dawn on me. "Do you think it's real? What she's saying about cults and sacrifices and that?"

"Oh, for sure," Bill said. "Happens all the time." I then saw his enthusiasm wane as he added, "Well, it used to."

Several hours into the journey, I noticed the scenery start to take on ever greater degrees of strangeness. We passed by old stately mansions of the early republic and still older colonial farmhouses, before emerging into a long, monotonous stretch of open shore country. The day was warm and sunny, but the landscape of sand, sedge-grass and stunted shrubbery seemed peculiarly desolate, and only became more so as we journeyed on. Small, weather-worn telephone poles lay beside the road, carrying only two frail wires, and now and then, we crossed crude, rotting bridges over tidal creeks that wound far inland and promoted the general isolation of the region.

Soon, our narrow course began to climb steeply, and I felt a singular sense of disquiet in looking at the lonely crest ahead where the rutted roadway met the sky. It was as if the van were about to keep on in its ascent, leaving the sane earth altogether and merging with the unknown arcana of the endless sky. The smell of the sea gently gained in strength until it had become a permanent fixture in the cabin, and I remember it producing rather an ominous taste in my mouth – if that makes any sense at all.

It was at this time that I decided to bring out my phone and do some preliminary research on Wikipedia. "Innsmouth is a seaport town on the coast of Essex County, Massachusetts, south of Plum Island and north of Cape Ann. Founded in 1643, noted for shipbuilding before the Revolution, and for being a seat of great marine prosperity in the early nineteenth—"

"What the fuck are you doing?" Bill barked, shooting me an evil eye.

"Reading out the Wikipedia page for Innsmouth," I replied. "I thought it might be useful to know a bit about the place."

"Maybe, but it's a bit fucking boring, ain't it?"

"Well, I don't know. I don't think so."

"How about you read it in your head?" Bill said. "Yeah, I'm charging you with the super special task of reading it all in your head, alright?"

"Okay," I replied.

"And for letting you do that, you can give me a backrub tonight – me muscles are gonna be sore as shit after all this driving."

After contemplating the arrangement for longer than I would care to admit, I promptly put away my phone. "I think I'm alright, actually."

Bill shrugged. "Your loss." He then slammed on the brakes so violently that I could not help but smack my head on the dashboard. "Careful!" Bill screamed as we screeched to a halt. "Don't want ya leaving any marks." He then rubbed the dashboard tenderly, wiping off the sweat I had left. "You alright, mate?" he spoke quietly into the van's aircon vents.

"What was that for?" I asked, unable to hide my anger, holding my throbbing head.

Bill pointed out the window to a gnarled tree by the side of the road, but I couldn't seem to understand how that satisfied my question.

"What about it?" I moaned.

"Look at it, you plonker," he replied. "It's got a bleeding sigil of Aegishjalmur on it."

"A sigil of what?"

"Aegishjalmur."

"And what's that?"

Bill stared at me in disbelief. "Are you joking?"

"About what?"

"Seriously, are you pulling my leg?"

"About what? About not knowing what that sigil is?"

"Yes. Jesus Christ, it's one of your three *basic* sigils of protection, yeah? Along with Algiz and Durex. You seriously don't know what a sigil of Aegishjalmur is?

I continued to look befuddled and shook my head.

Bill sighed a long and painful sigh. "What the hell do they teach you kids in schools these days? To put it simply, Todd – and I know you need stuff put simply – if we had passed by that tree, we'd have been full-on cursed. Like Kennedy-family cursed. Real dark shit. Someone clearly don't want no visitors."

Looking closer, the faint outline of a sigil carved into the bark slowly revealed itself. "How on earth did you spot—?"

BANG! BANG! BANG!

Clasping my ears, I turned to my side to see Bill leaning out the window, shooting at the sigil with his revolver. He went to shoot again, but the handgun jammed. He started smacking it, muttering to himself various insults only fit for an insentient weapon.

"You brought your gun?" I shouted, hands still pinned to my ears.

"Course," he shouted back. "Thought it could do with an outing. And it's already turned out pretty useful too, wouldn't ya say?"

"We could have just cut the bark, couldn't we?" I said as Bill leaned back into the van and started up the engine again. "You know, with a knife or something."

"Yeah, but what fun would that be?"

**

After haphazardly overtaking a dirty gray bus of extreme decrepitude as it slowly rattled up the road, we finally crested the valley and were rewarded with our first glimpse of fate-shadowed Innsmouth.

It was a large town of dense construction, yet one with a noticeable lack of visible life. From the tangle of chimney-pots scarcely drifted a wisp of smoke, and three tall steeples loomed stark and unpainted against the seaward horizon. One of them was crumbling down at the top, and in that and another there were only black gaping holes where clock-dials should have been. The vast huddle of sagging gambrel roofs and peaked gables conveyed with offensive clearness the idea of wormy decay, and as we approached along the, now descending, road I could see that many roofs had wholly caved in. There were some large square Georgian houses too, with hipped roofs, cupolas, and railed widow's walks, and stretching inland from the town I noticed the gleaming, steel line of a new railway.

It was as if we were stepping back in time.

"Jesus, what a shithole," Bill muttered. "Sort of looks familiar though. Think I might've come here once as a kid."

"Oh yeah?" I asked vacantly, strangely allured by the grim panorama in front of me.

"Yeah," Bill replied with a faint but noticeable wobble in his voice. "With me dad. On a job."

The decay of the town was worst close to the waterfront. The harbor, long clogged with sand, was enclosed by an ancient stone breakwater; on which I could begin to discern the minute forms of a few seated fishermen, and at whose end were what looked like the foundations of a bygone lighthouse. A sandy tongue had formed inside this barrier, and upon it I saw a few decrepit cabins, moored dories, and scattered lobster-pots. The only deep water seemed to be where the river poured out past the belfried structure and turned southward to join the ocean at the breakwater's end.

Here and there, the ruins of wharves jutted out from the shore to end in indeterminate rottenness, those farthest south seeming the most decayed. And far out at sea, joined to the port by a thin stretch of miniature railway along a fresh wooden pier, upon which I could see a small, pretend steam train, I glimpsed a long, black line of rock with a plain, boxy building sat atop it. We would later come to learn this repulsive rock feature was known to locals as Devil Reef, and several decades ago had been involved in a failed business venture that sought to convert it into a tourist attraction. God knows who thought that a good idea.

We met no one on the road down and into the town, but presently began to pass deserted farms in varying stages of ruin. I noticed a few inhabited houses with rags stuffed in the broken windows and shells and dead fish lying about in littered yards. Once or twice I saw listless-looking people working in barren gardens or digging clams on the fishy-smelling beach below, and groups of dirty children playing around weed-grown doorsteps. Somehow, these people seemed more disquieting than the dismal buildings, for almost every one had certain peculiarities of posture and motions which I instinctively disliked without being able to define or comprehend them.

"Holy guacamole, these guys look like freaks," Bill said, eyeballing the locals left and right as we made our way with much haste towards the center. "Welcome to Innsmouth, I guess."

Chapter Four.

Our first port of call was to the Holiday Inn where we planned to check into our room and leave the van before beginning our investigations.

We pulled into the yard of broken cobble that served as a parking lot, and locking the van, headed into the hotel. It was a tall, cupola-crowned building with remnants of yellow paint, old and worn, and the only aspect of it which seemed to have been updated in the past fifty years was the Holiday Inn sign which leant awkwardly outside in the unkempt grass. Passing into the lobby, I noticed a rotting wooden placard nearly entirely engulfed by a bush – it read, 'Gilman House'.

Inside the spectral establishment, there was only one person in sight – an elderly woman who had a fishy look about her. And by that, I don't mean suspicious. I mean literally fish-like. She had a queer narrow head with a flat nose, and bulgy, starry eyes that never seemed to shut. A receding forehead and chin graced her face with an eccentricity beyond compare, and her ears were singularly undeveloped. Her skin was also most perplexing – rough and scabby, with the sides of her neck all shriveled and creased. She also appeared to have the misfortune of approaching total baldness. All in all, not the most attractive woman I had ever seen.

I noticed Bill holding back some reaction – whether that was to be laughter or gagging, I'm not quite sure. On approaching the desk, a disgusting seaweed stench stopped the both of us from taking another step.

"Jesus Christ," Bill muttered to me out the side of his mouth. "Someone needs to wash down there, if you know what I mean."

I shot Bill a look hoping to relay the message that he should keep his voice down lest we create trouble for ourselves we sorely did not need.

"Alright, lady," Bill began. The woman slowly looked up to the pair of us with those watery-blue unblinking eyes. I found myself swallowing in nervous anticipation. "Me and my buddy here have booked a room for the night. We'd like to check in if that ain't too much trouble."

"The woom in't weddy wet," the woman croaked in a voice like sandpaper and glue. "And the cweaner's been feewing ill, so it might not be weady today at all. You might as well weave now."

"Well, hopefully she'll feel better later," Bill replied dubiously. "We can leave the van outside though, yeah?"

The woman seemed displeased at our inclination to stay. "Cars are vewy ofen stowen wound here. I suggest you weave instead."

"Well, we're not gonna leave. We've got shit to do, so just keep an eye on it for us."

"I'm vewy bizzie. It will pwobabwee be stown. I suggest weaving."

"Jesus Christ," Bill leaned in to read her name tag, "Brenda. We're not leaving. Stop trying to get us to leave. I booked a room at your prestigious establishment for a reason. Now, we're parking the van here and I expect our room to be ready by the evening or I'll be making some very serious complaints with the higher ups, alright?"

Brenda stared unblinkingly at Bill, severely unimpressed.

"Come on, Todd," Bill said, grabbing my arm. "Let's get to it."

***

"What was up with that woman's face?" I asked as we trekked towards our client's address.

"Dunno. Probs some degenerative disease or something. Don't remember anyone looking like that when I came as a kid – and I think I'd remember."

As we turned a corner, we came face to face with a gaggle of just as odd-looking people shuffling along the pavement. Their crouching, shambling gait was most off-putting, but the golden jewlry hanging around their necks, wrists, and ankles was most alluring. So weird and strange were the adornments that they almost seemed like the work of an alien race far more advanced than our own. Before I could get a better glimpse, however, the group quickly scuffled past us and round the corner out of sight.

"Did you see those bracelets?" I asked.

"Huh?" Bill said, shaking his head and blinking rapidly as if awakening from a dream.

"Their jewelry," I replied. "Did you see it? It was so… so strange. And shiny."

"Sorry, mate, not gonna lie to ya, I was thinking about that freak back in the hotel – I was wondering how desperate I'd have to be, ya know?"

After a brief and disturbing conversation with far too much detail for my liking, we soon found ourselves outside the client's house. It was one of the better houses we had come across in Innsmouth, though that wasn't saying much, and I believe in any other town it would have stuck out like a sore, infected thumb.

Bill rang the doorbell and we patiently waited. There was no response. My mind began to race with possibilities both fair and foul.

Bill rang the doorbell again, but a disgusting and raspy voice shouted to us from one of the upstairs windows of the house opposite. We spun around. "You won't find her in there," the hidden voice explained from behind a thick sheet of rotting curtain. "She's gone out to look for her husband."

"Cheers, mate," Bill replied, shooting the window a thumbs up, before turning back to me, and instantly switching demeanor. "Well, that's just bloody brilliant," he said with a snarl. "I told her I'd be here at nine – what's she playing at?"

"Nine?" I said, startled. I checked the time on my phone. "But it's three."

"Yeah, I know," Bill replied smugly. "I always tell people a little earlier than I'm actually gonna be, don't I? It's a power move. Makes them respect you more – read that little tip in a sociology book." He then looked up and down the street in a lazy last ditch effort before rubbing his stomach. "Are you hungry? I'm hungry."

"I could eat," I said ambivalently. "But shouldn't we, you know, look for our contact?"

"Just getting a little snack, Todd. Jeez, chill out, mate. This is our first ever job together – let's have a good time, yeah?"

"But there's a sacrificial cult on the loose, isn't there?"

"And it'll still be there after lunch, won't it? So, there's nothing to worry about. Now, I fancy a Mickey D's. You?"

I let out a little snigger at Bill's hopeful suggestion. "Bill, I don't think they're going to have a McDonalds here."

"Oh, ye of little faith," Bill replied smugly.

***

Rounding the corner, the large golden arches blazed so brightly in contrast to the rest of the dingy, run-down town that it almost appeared to be a protrusion from another, more heavenly dimension.

The building was a large pillared hall, and its once white paint was now grey and peeling.

"Here we go," Bill said fervently, rubbing his greedy hands together. "Nuggets and fries. Nuggets and fries. Here we go, boys."

"I can't believe it," I replied.

My attention, however, was stolen by the raucous tones of a cracked bell across the street. The sound came from a squat-towered stone church built in a clumsy Gothic fashion and having a disproportionately high basement with shuttered windows. Though the hands of its clock were missing on the side I glimpsed, I could only infer it to be running slow or fast as my phone showed the time to be 3:23pm. Then suddenly all thoughts of time were blotted out by an onrushing image of sharp intensity and unaccountable horror which had seized me before I knew what it really was. The door of the church basement was open, revealing a rectangle of blackness inside. And as I looked, a certain object crossed, or seemed to cross, that dark rectangle; burning into my brain a momentary conception of nightmare which was all the more maddening because analysis could not reveal a single nightmarish quality in it.

It was a living object – and had I been in a steadier mood I would have found nothing whatsoever of terror in it. Clearly, as I realized a moment later, it was most likely the pastor of the church or a janitor. I slowed my breathing and told myself to show more restraint in my fearful flights of fancy. If I was losing my nerves at the sight of a priest crossing a doorway, how would I react when face to face with the real enemy?

Grabbing my arm, and yanking me towards the McDonalds, Bill stared at me in a fashion that seemed almost caring. "You alright, mate? You look like you've seen a ghost." I nodded to show I was fine, and at this reassurance, Bill revealed his true intentions. "Alright, cool beans, 'cos I'm gonna need you to cover this one – ain't got no cash on me."

"That's fine, I'll just pay with my phone," I said.

"I don't think this is the sort of place you can barter like that, Todd." Just then, I glimpsed out the corner of my eye, an old black and gold sign on the wall of the restaurant that I could only with great difficulty make out the words on. It read: 'Esoteric Order of Dagon'.

I pointed the sign out to Bill. "Oh no," he said. "That's not good."

"What?" I enquired. "Do you know it?"

"Nah, it just doesn't sound good, does it? Esoteric. Dagon. Order. They just don't vibe well together, do they?" I couldn't help but agree. "Anyway," he shrugged. "Stop working. We're on break."

Inside the building, we were once again only greeted by a single person – this one, however, to my great relief, was a vaguely normal-looking teen. Bill strode on over and wasted no time in getting to business. "Twenty nugs, large fries, Coke, and this guy's paying." He jabbed his thumb at me.

"And I'll have a filet-o-fish, please." Bill shot me a look as if I had just passed wind.

"Who the fuck orders the filet-o-fish?"

"I'm afraid we're actually all out of those," the teen nervously announced.

Bill grinned and, turning back to her, asked, "Not even bothering to stock it anymore? Smart."

"No, it's actually all the locals eat," she replied. "We're all cleaned out."

Bill recoiled in horror, his face draining of color. "Todd, we need to get the fuck out of here. Fast. This place is sick — truly sick."

"I'll just have ten nuggets and a medium fries then," I said, ignoring Bill's melodramatic turn of character. "Thanks."

She nodded and prodded in the order. Bill collapsed at a table by the window, head in hands, and began muttering to himself. I paid and joined him.

"There is something seriously wrong with this town," he said.

"I know but I think their obsession with fish filets are the least of our worries."

Bill pursed his lips. "Not a good sign though."

"Why don't we ask her if she knows anything?" I suggested, nodding my head towards the counter girl.

"She works in a McDonalds," Bill scoffed. "What's she gonna know? How to flip a burger?"

"Well, she lives in the town, doesn't she? And she seems, you know, actually normal. She might be able to help us."

Bill shook his head, laughing to himself. "You young liberals. *So* progressive. What next? Ask the janitor for help with some quantum physics?" He gargled for five seconds.

"I really think we should ask," I continued. "What harm could it do?"

"Alright, how about this?" Bill responded, a smile creeping onto his face. "I'll let you play detective and ask your little questions to the fast food worker, if…" Bill's grin grew sardonic and lingered a little too long for my liking.

"If…?" I questioned. Bill nodded, clearly enjoying the little game. "If what?"

"You know," he smirked.

Suddenly, it hit me. "If I rub your back tonight…" I sighed.

"Bingo!"

"Fine," I said. "If I must."

"Bloody hell," Bill said, the tone of his voice somewhere between pleasantly surprised and begrudgingly impressed. "You really are a keen bean."

"Well, yes, this is important, isn't it? Peoples' lives are at stake. And, you know, maybe it's got something to do with the humanity-saving business I was told about."

"Oh yeah, your weird dream — forgot about that. Just got used to you being here." Bill turned to look out the grimy window that displayed a most portentous portrait. "Feels like you've always been with me."

I found this admission strangely endearing, but before I could push the subject any further, the young woman came over with our food. Bill nodded to me – a sign of permission – so I took a deep breath and readied myself for my first interrogation.

"Are you from around here?" I asked as she placed our tray down and Bill instantly tore into the nuggets.

"No, no," she laughed, with an overtone of profound gratitude. "No, I got transferred here – unfortunately."

"Do you know anything about a sacrificial cult operating in the town?" I asked.

"Ooh," Bill groaned, shaking his head. "You never dive right in like that, mate. You gotta build up a rapport first." He turned to the girl. "Sorry, excuse my friend. How are your parents? Are you on your period?"

The girl looked over the pair of us with a terribly bewildered expression. "I don't know anything about a cult; my parents are fine, thanks; and I'm not answering that last one."

"What's up with the locals' weird fucking fish faces?" Bill asked, stuffing a handful of fries into his mouth.

At this, the girl laughed. "I don't know. There are a lot of very tight knit families around here, if you know what I mean. I assume it's something to do with that. But I try not to think about it, to be honest. I just avoid them as much as I can. Like, there are some normal-looking people around too, but it does seem to be getting more and more... weird."

"And you haven't noticed anything that could be maybe a little cultish?" I asked. "Or seen any kidnappings or anything like that?"

"No," she replied, shaking her head. "When I'm not at work, I'm in my room. I spend as little time outside as physically possible."

"Smart girl," Bill replied.

"Do you know anyone who might know more about the town?" I pressed on. "Who might know more about strange goings on?"

"What? Like conspiracy-type stuff?"

"Yeah, exactly."

"Well…" She hesitated, clearly trying to decide whether to tell us or not.

"Come on," Bill interrupted. "Spill the beans, girlfriend."

"There is this one, like, crackhead woman I pass on the way back from work most days. She's always, like, spouting off about conspiracy stuff. She might be able to help you."

Bill jumped up from the table. "Perfect!" As me and the girl stared on, baffled, Bill undid his laces, took off his shoe, and pulled from inside, a crumpled ball of paper. Unwrapping the paper, he revealed a single rock of crack. "This should get her talking then!"

Chapter Five.

Bill handed the crazed woman his crack rock. She clutched onto it as if her own child. "Oh, bless ye. Bless ye," she said through a strained voice. Although she did not have (what I shall now dub in the most novel fashion) 'the Innsmouth look', she was certainly still an exceptionally odd-looking woman in her own way. Well, perhaps not really in her own way – in the way every crackhead old woman looks.

"Now, tell us everything you know about this shithole," Bill said, crossing his arms. "This is a trade, remember? I'm no charity."

"Everything?" she asked, sniffing the crack in one hand, and pulling on her wild, matted, greasy hair with the other.

"Todo," Bill replied before turning to me proudly. "That means everything in Spanish!" He smiled with the boastfulness of a five year old child who had just eaten an entire box of crayons.

"Listen in and listen close then," she said, "because there's much to say, and half of it ye won't believe — so sick and twisted as it is." We leant in, ready to learn the truth of this corrupted place. "Mockingbird. Mockingbird is the key. The great reckoning is coming, oh, believe me! The light shall conquer after the storm. Ye know it to be true, in your heart of hearts! Ye know it! Ye know it!" With glee, she laid a gnarled claw on my shoulder, and whispered, "The Clintons will finally fall. Hanks will be brought to justice. Epstein and his 'suicide' will be revealed for the assassination it truly was." The old woman's whisper grew fainter, and I found myself shuddering at the terrible and sincere portentousness of her intonation. "He knew too much, he knew too much…" Here the old woman faltered, mumbled, and lapsed into a moody and apprehensive silence; before leaping back into a hysterical frenzy. "Oh, ye children! Listen! Listen, it gets deep! Deeper than any of ye could imagine. Satanic pedophilic rituals sustain the capital — it is the lifeblood of the senate! Sick, sick, sick. Adrenochrome is what they're after, yes! Yes, adrenochrome — they take if from the glands of children, you know? Children! Can ye imagine? Children! They wish to be forever young! Immortal demons!"

Her moon-gray eyes were almost savage and maniacal now, and her rotting teeth seemed to wobble with excitement. She probably saw me shrink in fear, for she began to cackle evilly. "He he he! Now ye see! Now ye see! The Rothschilds — originators, all

– oh so long ago. Nothing changes. Nothing ever changes, but everything! Everything! The cabal cries its death cry! The air sings with its G-G-G-G-G corruption! The air stings! No more! No more! The darkness is nearly over, I tell ye! The great awakening! We are all a part of it! Whether ye want to be or not, ye are a part of it!" The old woman was panting now, and perspiring profusely. Her grip on my shoulder tightened. "Where we go one, we go all! Remember that. Remember that. And Princess Di – don't forget her! Killed for daring to oppose the great attack on the twin towers! Remember that! Never forget. Never forget. Anonymous voices whisper truth where faces can only lie!"

She was really screaming now, and the mad frenzy of her voice disturbed me more than I care to own. "Oh, Q! Oh, Q! The rapture shall wipe this country clean!" She began to laugh manically again, her vicelike grip shaking in a mad terror. "He he he! Ye don't believe me, do ye? Then explain this! Explain why I was left to rot by my own family after learning the truth! Explain why they would do that if they weren't under the control of the great devil Beelzebub! He he he! Ye can't, can ye? But I cannot support child eating. Child feasting, no less! Better to be alone and righteous than loved and wicked! What say ye? What say ye?" She glanced nervously over her shoulder and then turned back to stare at me in a most solemn and thoughtful fashion. "The battle is underground, my friend. The war behind curtains." And then, charging back up into a momentous howl, she screamed, "Shadowed conflicts all abound! He he he! Ye know! Ye know! The Clinton's time is ripe! The storm approaches! The storm shall wipe—!"

***

"Well, that was a fucking waste of time," Bill said as we meandered back to the center of town. "And good crack," he added somberly.

"I mean, what did you expect?" I replied.

"Hard truths. Hard truths are what I expected. Truths that make people go mad. Truths that make people turn to crack." He jabbed his thumb behind him. "I knew all that, already." He sighed, shaking his head. "Disappointing. Just bloody disappointing. A real poor performance from her. Nothing like the crackheads we used to have – they were founts of knowledge, they were. For a lick of your shoe, they'd tell ya anything you could ask for. They knew all the goings on. All the history of a place. And they were just a bloody good laugh." He sighed again, and I noticed a wistful look in his eyes. A look conveying more than he was letting on. "Well, there's nothing for it, I guess. We're just gonna have to break into our contact's house."

"What?" I spurted out. "Break in?"

"Well, yeah. Why not? What else have we got to do till dinner?"

***

Sneaking around the back of the house, Bill spotted a glass window on the second floor he believed he could throw me through if he balanced on top of an upside down wheelbarrow.

"I'm not doing that," I protested.

"Why not?"

"Why not? Why won't I allow myself to be hurled through a glass pane window?"

"Yeah."

"Because I'll get seriously injured."

"Nah, you won't. You'll be fine. Anyway, I thought you said this was important? I thought you said peoples' lives were at stake? Surely that's worth being thrown through one small window."

"This is stupid," I said. "I'm not doing it."

"What if I throw a rock through it first and break the glass for ya? What about that?"

"Still no," I said, breathless in disbelief. "Are you insane?"

"What did you just say to me?"

"I said 'Are you insane?'"

In a flash, Bill lunged at me and grabbed me by the collar. "I'm as sane as they come, motherfucker. I'm the stablelist person there ever was. I'm stabler than a tabler. Alright?" Bill was shaking uncontrollably now, his lip madly quivering, and his eyelids fluttering at a pace I never before thought possible. For the sake of his health, I resolved to cease the conflict.

"Alright, I'll do it," I said. "You're not mad. I'll do it."

At this, Bill dropped me and stepped back, instantly resuming his usual happy-go-lucky demeanor. "Sweet. Cool beans, cool beans." He stooped down and picked up a loose brick. "This should do the trick." He then hurled the brick at the window, smashing through the glass. A chorus of nearby dogs began barking, and I instinctively cowered, expecting to be told off by some parent or teacher within seconds. "Did you see that?" Bill shouted with astonishment. "Old man's still got it. Weren't that the best throw you've ever seen?"

I nodded, not wishing to make any more noise than necessary. "Alright, come here," he said, beckoning me over as he pushed the wheelbarrow towards the window. "Your turn."

I skulked towards him, and taking me by surprise, he effortlessly scooped me up and mounted the wheelbarrow. "Alright, on the count of three, okay?" I nodded once again, feeling I had no other option than complete cooperation. "Alright. Three. Two."

Bill then jumped and lobbed me through the broken window. "One." Although I did in fact make it into the building, I also succeeded in cutting myself quite severely on the shards of broken glass that still rested on the window sill.

Bleeding rather freely, I limped down the stairs and opened up the back door for Bill. With one cursory glance to my injuries, Bill strode into the house and began his investigations. "Try not to bleed on the carpet too much – don't wanna get charged if they have to redo it."

"I'm actually in quite a lot of pain, Bill," I whimpered. "Bleeding on the carpet is the least of my concerns. I think I'm really quite injured." Dropping to my knees, I clutched my gashes, but they stung too much to hold for long.

"You're fine, mate," Bill shouted from the kitchen where I could hear him pouring a glass of water. He then drifted back out to the corridor and proceeded to glug the drink while standing over my huddled figure. "Come on. Get up."

"Bill, I'm in real pain."

Bill half-laughed, half-huffed. "What the hell do you know about real pain? *I* know real pain. I know real pain, and I'm telling ya, it's not a few little cuts." He huffed again. "Jesus, I've known more pain than you can imagine. I've had a Leng spider lay a thousand pulsating eggs in me knee. How d'you think that felt? Had to raise the bloody things too… Saying goodbye was the part that hurt the most."

"What the fuck are you on about?" I said, feeling my head go faint. "Bill, I really think I need help."

"For Christ's sake, wait here then." Bill marched back into the kitchen and came back a minute later with several old tea towels, which he quickly used to bandage up my injuries. "There you go. You all better now?" he asked, with more than an undercurrent of condescension. "Is little Todd all better now?"

I brushed him off, getting to my feet, and leaning on the wall to stop from falling over. "Let's just look around and get out of here."

"That's the idea," Bill said. "You check downstairs, I'll go up."

We got to work, but as Bill ascended the stairs, I could hear him muttering to himself, "Jesus, he got blood everywhere. We better not have to pay for this."

An hour went by in a languid daze before anything eventful happened. "Todd! Todd!" Bill shouted from an upstairs bedroom. "I found her husband's friggen diary!"

Limping up the stairs, I soon found Bill kneeling down beside a bed, and holding in his hands a worn leather book. "I reckon this has got what we need to know."

Bill was right. The diary was most illuminating, and here I shall transcribe the pages as best I can remember.

November 10th, 1971

Hello, Diary.

It's me, your owner: Gregather, aged 12. I shall write in you every day. That's a promise. I shall tell you every important thing that ever happens to me. My first kiss. My first dance. My first fight. My first vinyl. We shall become best of friends, diary! I can't wait for all we will share!

February 23rd, 1985

Ha. I just found this diary again after all these years. Look how well that promise turned out. Well, this time I mean it. I'm going to keep you updated of everything that's going on in my life and this bustling town.

Let's start with a little snapshot of Innsmouth. Things are actually going in the right direction for once! Local businesses are growing well. The people seem to have a gentle, happy mood about them — and it seems that all our past unpleasantness is behind us. Mother and Father desperately wished to escape this little coastal town when they were alive, but I wish they could see it now.

I remember as a child, late at night, after a drink or two, Father used to whisper dangerous secrets about this place and its history to me. Secrets about powerful old cults, and Esoteric Orders of Dagon or Dogan or some other strange name. He said shadowy figures used to run the town until they were all arrested and thrown out by the FBI — on what exact charge, he never said. I used to think he was making it all up just to scare me like parents are prone to do, but after talking it through with friends, I found theirs had also told them similar tales.

Just like mine, their parents had whispered in the dead of night about Obed Marsh and his deal with the devils who lived deep under the sea. About how Devil Reef held portals to a great underwater city, from which Obed retrieved weird and elaborate gold jewelry.

Anyway, however much truth is behind these stories — and I doubt there's much — it's all behind us now. We shouldn't worry our heads with such things. We should just jam out to crazy cassette tapes, and enjoy this magical thing we call life!

And what's new with me? Well, I've met this beautiful woman and I think I'm going to ask for her hand in marriage. Wish me luck, diary! If she accepts, I shall be the luckiest man in the world.

April 18th, 2007

I really need to get better at this diary-keeping business. Anyway, what's occurred since we last spoke?

Well, unfortunately, the town's been changing — and not in a good way. Big business have muscled their way in here, shutting down local shops and restaurants left, right, and center. It's a real shame. This town is becoming the same as any other.

And something about the people in the town has been changing as well. We've been getting lots of new folk immigrating into Innsmouth, and there's just something off about them. It's hard to explain, and I don't want to come off as racist or anything, but they've all got strange faces and they talk weird — and they don't interact with us locals at all. They keep to themselves.

Each to their own, I guess.

Oh, and remember that woman I was going to ask to marry me? Well, she declined but a year later I asked someone else and they accepted! Looking back, I'm actually quite glad — the one I was going to ask has not aged well.

I've also decided, on the advice of a close friend to invest all my savings on the stock market! Although I've made some poor investing decisions in the past (such as that damned Devil Reef tourist attraction — what a complete and utter failure that was), I'm pretty confident with this one. My friend says the market has been on a 'bull run' recently and he's given me his guarantee that it'll last at least the next few years so here's to him and a better future for us all!

Also, I've got a Zune which is absolutely amazing. It can store thousands of songs on it and it fits in my pocket! WTF! Technology, eh!

Oh yeah, also I've got a 20 year old kid now. He's alright. Until next time, diary.

October 13th, 2018
Hello again. Long time no write.

Innsmouth has changed. A lot. It's become a deeply weird and depressing place. Remember those weird immigrants I wrote about last time? Well, they've taken over the town. Us old locals are the minority now — and it seems like every year, there's less and less of us, and more and more of them.

My son — he went missing last month, and we haven't been able to contact him. No one knows what's happened to him, and the police haven't been much help. They pinned it down to him running away, but I know my son, and he wouldn't have done that. Lots of people have been randomly disappearing over the last few years. Yes, something's going on, and I think it's got everything to do with the foreign freaks who have taken over this town.

Also, looking back at my previous entry, I was reminded of my devastating investment decision, and that's put me in the right mind this time to NOT invest in this Ethereum thing that same friend has been telling me about. 'Sure thing', my ass! I've learnt my lesson.

Anyway, I'm going to pop on my 'chill beats to investigate to' playlist and go out looking for answers. If no one else is going to do it, I guess it falls on my shoulders. Wish me luck, diary!

January 22nd, 2019

The Deep Ones are returning…

Over the past few months, I have learnt much. There is a cult at work in this town, sacrificing locals and receiving rewards in the form of fucked up jewelry. It's those foreign weirdo scum. They're the ones that killed my son.

And guess what, diary? I'm going to kill them now. The Deep Ones. Those devil children. Our town's past is coming back to haunt us. Back then, we simply treated the symptoms, not the disease. And now it's come to take revenge – though in a smarter fashion; staying in the shadows.

The Deep Ones are returning! The Deep Ones are returning!

My wife thinks I'm mad, but she spends her days watching Real Housewives so what the heck does she know? I've been investigating. I know the truth.

I know these dirty capitalist Dagon-worshiping scum think a nice necklace is worth as much as my son's life. I'm going to show them how wrong they are. I'm going to wipe their ugly murdering mugs off the face of this planet.

Until next time, diary. Until my victory.

"Holy mother of God," Bill muttered, turning the page to reveal only a blank double spread. "This guy's diary keeping was sporadic as fuck. Five entries in nearly fifty years? And twenty years between two of 'em? That's mental. Just absolutely mental."

"But what about what he was actually saying?" I asked. "What about The Deep Ones? What's that about?"

"Oh yeah, that was pretty wild too, I guess." Bill stood up, pocketing the journal. "Probs got something to do with the Esoteric Order of Dagon, that's my guess. Pretty useful, really. This guy's basically figured everything out for us." He then stretched out his arms, yawning. "You fancy a Mickey D's again?"

Chapter Six.

"She must have got taken by them too then," I said, tucking into a Big Mac.

"Yeah," Bill replied quietly, looking overly troubled by the suggestion.

"What?" I asked.

"Do you think we'll still get our money? I mean, I didn't find no cash stash when I was looking round the house. Do you think she set up an ACH payment or something?"

"Probably not," I said.

Bill's head dropped. "Thought so. Typical. Just bloody typical." He dipped a nugget in sauce and chewed on it soberly. "We'll have to just break in again after we've done the job and you can maybe try hacking into her bank or something like that and sending the funds over."

"I don't think I could do that," I replied honestly. "And, even if I could, I don't think I would."

"Who knows, maybe she'll just show up anyway. Maybe she just went on a nice weekend break." Bill then eyed my bandages and I noticed a twinkle of remorse in his eye. "How ya feeling?"

"Pretty bad."

"Fair." Bill sucked on his Coke, loudly slurping as he finished the drink. "I did throw you a little hard, I'll admit that. Just don't know me own strength sometimes."

I sighed. "It's alright. I'll live."

"Yeah, you will, won't you? You may not look it but you're a tough bugger." He then leant over the table and ruffled my hair, inducing a warm, sort of fuzzy feeling inside.

"What's the plan then?" I asked, a little embarrassed and eager to move on.

"Head back to the hotel, rest up, and get back on it tomorrow morning. What d'ya think?"

"Sounds good." I smiled.

"Let's get a McFlurry for the road then!" Bill shouted, fizzing with glee. "I think we've earned it!"

***

Outside the hotel, congregated around the door, were a group of suspicious looking fellows – all with the Innsmouth look.

"Don't make eye contact with 'em," Bill whispered out the side of his mouth as he put his head down and marched through the middle of the small crowd. I followed suit but could still feel their many bulging, watery eyes staring at the pair of us with an odd intensity.

Once inside, the receptionist reluctantly gave us the keys to our room – not once blinking, I feel I should mention – and we made our way up the stairs and down the partially-lit corridor to where we would be trying to sleep that night. The cleaner, it seemed, had made a miraculous recovery.

"Do you think they could've been part of the Esoteric Order of Dagon?" I asked as Bill tried to unlock our door.

"Speaking from experience, I've found it's best not to think too hard about things. Don't try to understand what's happening or predict nothing. Just react to what's happening right in front of ya, and keep your mind blank the rest of the time – only way to live, far as I see." Bill then gave up trying to unlock the door and just gave it a good shove. It swung open.

At first sight, our room appeared rather dismal. On closer inspection, it only became more so. There were peculiar stains on the ceiling, broken springs sticking out of the dirty, thin double mattress we would be sharing, and the lock for the door appeared to be situated on the floor as if it had recently been unscrewed.

The windows overlooked a dingy courtyard hemmed in by low, deserted brick blocks, and from this floor, we were burdened with a view of the decrepit westward-stretching roofs of the sickening town.

In the corner of the room was a bathroom – a discouraging antique with an ancient marble bowl, a tin tub, a single dim bulb, and musty, rotting, wooden paneling around all the plumbing fixtures.

"Not bad," Bill said, surveying the room, hands on hips.

"Not bad?"

"I've stayed in worse. If I've got a roof over me head, I'm happy."

At that moment, the ceiling partially collapsed, coating half the bed in plaster and rainwater. Bill jumped on the other half. "Shotgun this side."

The old telephone on the desk then presently rang, and we both looked at one another, wondering who it could possibly be. Bill gestured for me to answer with a wave of the hand, so I did, placing it on speakerphone. "Hello?" I said.

"How's your woom?"

"Well, the ceiling—"

"Fine, thanks." Bill shouted from the bed, interrupting me.

"You don't want to make a compwaint?"

"Nah, it's fine."

There was a moment of silence before the lady continued, "Are you… Are you sure? There are spwings sticking out of the bed. And the lock on the door's bwoken."

"And the ceiling's just collapsed," I added.

"That's alright, we'll live." Bill placed his arms behind his head and looked as happy as Larry

"Hmm… Hold on." We then heard the sound of the lady's footsteps walking away from the phone, and thirty seconds later, approaching it again. She picked back up the receiver. "Twy the water in your bathwoom."

Bill nodded to me, and so I went over and tried the sink. Nothing came out of the faucet. "Nothing," I said.

"It's not working," Bill relayed.

"Ah, bwilliant. Well, you won't be wanting to stay without wunning water then. I'll awange a wefund for you and you can be on your way."

"Nah, it's alright," Bill interrupted. "I'm on this no-washing-your-hair fad anyway. And it's only for one night. Cheers for checking in though."

"So, you're staying?" she asked with bewilderment.

"Yep."

"...On your head be it then." She abruptly hung up.

Bill and I both stared at the phone, not knowing quite what to make of the situation. "That last bit sounded quite ominous," I said.

"I'll tell you what sounds ominous," he replied, beginning to undo his sweaty shirt. "It's time for me backrub." And groaning, he turned himself over.

Although massaging Bill's hairy and surprisingly mole-infested back wasn't the most pleasant experience, I appreciated the distraction. I felt it advisable to keep my mind wholesomely occupied, for I felt it would not do well to brood over the abnormalities of the ancient, blight-shadowed town I had experienced that day whilst still within its borders.

After Bill was satisfied, he then moved over to the desk and swiped everything off it like a particularly attention-starved cat. Then laying out his revolver and bullets, he proceeded to work on inscribing strange runes into all of them – though precisely what carvings he was making, I could not tell for every time I went to take a look, he would cover them with his body and tell me to mind my beeswax.

Before bed, and after Bill was done, I dragged the desk in front of the door to serve as a rudimentary lock. Bill called me every inventive variation of 'cowardly' under the sun, but I felt it better to be safe than sorry – and by that time, I had become very practiced at not taking Bill's insults to heart.

After giving my teeth a dry brush, as the water was still being shy, I came back out to find Bill already fast asleep, snoring with his mouth wide open. After brushing aside the detritus on my half of the bed, and drying it as best I could with a towel, I slowly and carefully got in beside him, not wishing to awaken the slumbering beast.

I laid there in the dark for many an hour, water periodically dripping on my face, though for precisely how long, I could not tell you. My mind raced with images and fascinations. What had happened to the couple who invited us here? How were the Esoteric Order of Dagon operating? Would they come for us? How come Bill had no problem sleeping here but seemed so restless at home? And how was all of this linked to Pickman's enigmatic grand plan? Were we somehow to be the saviors of humanity?

With these endless questions whirling round my head, I drifted off into a half-sleep where I dreamt a series of strange visions indeed. I was unceremoniously expelled from these dreams, however, by the sound of the stairs and corridors creaking at intervals as if with footsteps. There were no voices, and it struck me that there was something subtly furtive about the creaking. As you can imagine, this was rather off-putting, and I debated whether I should even try to get back to sleep.

In the darkness, every faint noise of the night seemed magnified, and a flood of doubly unpleasant thoughts swept over me. After a long, dreary interval of sustained dread, there came the fresh creaking of the corridor – this time closer and clearer. Then came that soft, damnably unmistakable sound which seemed like a malign fulfilment of all my apprehensions. Without the least shadow of a doubt, the handle on our door was being turned.

I quickly turned over to Bill and began rapidly tapping him. "Bill," I whispered, my voice vibrating with terror. "Bill. Bill."

The door was being pushed but the desk I had propped against it was working well as a barrier. "Bill," I muttered louder.

"Jackie," he mumbled back, still asleep. "Don't go. Don't go… Don't go down Park Street this time of day, it'll be rammed. I'm telling ya."

"Bill, wake up. Wake up."

I could now make out the terrifying sound of a multitude of voices on the other side of the door –

though to call them voices does those horrific sounds no justice. They were hoarse barkings and loose-syllabled croakings that bore insanely little resemblance to recognized human speech.

I was in a desperate panic now and so resorted to shaking Bill violently. He snapped awake, and suddenly seemed so alert that one would imagine sleep was but a distant memory to him. "What is it?" he asked.

I pointed to the door and the slowly moving desk with a trembling finger. "They're trying to get in," I whispered.

"Oh right, fair dinkums." He then rolled over and snuggled tight with the duvet, ready to return to sleep.

"Bill!" I shouted, shoving him again. "We need to do something!" The attempts on the door then doubled in aggressiveness, and so I grabbed the duvet and threw it off him.

"Hey!" Bill protested as I ran to the door and shoved the desk back against it, eliminating the little progress our invaders had made. I then felt them barge against it violently, all attempts at secrecy now moot. Bill stroppily got out of bed and meandered over to me as I held the fort. "Don't worry, mate. I've got this." He then winked at me before stepping back and shouting, "Hey, guys. Don't wowwy about it, I've killed them alweady. Just eating them now. Yum, yum, yum. You guys can go home now."

Despite Bill's miraculous performance, the invaders continued in their attempts to break into our room.

"Have you got a plan B?"

"Course, mate." Bill leant into my ear and whispered, "We should jump out the window."

"Out the window? We're four stories up — and it's just straight down." I was now feeling complete and absolute despair, and a wave of ghastly horror swept through me as I contemplated the very real possibility of this being the end for me.

Bill then tried a connecting door leading to a room adjacent ours but, to my total despair, it was locked. "We'll go through here," he said. "There's a sloped roof we can drop onto on the other side."

"Jesus fucking Christ," I wailed as I reorientated my footing to push back harder against our intruders' increasingly desperate attempts to break in. Bill then ran back from the connecting door, spun around, and sprinted full on at it, leaping into the air at the last second, connecting his foot with the lock and breaking cleanly through into the next room.

I let go of the desk and dashed through the broken door with him. Bill was already opening the window, and behind me, I could hear hideous gruntings and subdued barkings as the intruders pushed the desk aside and wormed into our room.

"Quick!" I screamed.

Bill stopped and turned around. "Oh, good note, mate. Yeah, I was taking me time with it but, yeah, now you've said it, I think I'll actually get a move on now. Seriously — great fucking idea. I dunno how it slipped my mind."

"Bill!" I screamed as I snapped my head behind me and saw those disgusting creatures standing in the connecting doorway. The one at the front had an abominably large and heavily veined head, with a hideous greyish-blue tinge to his skin that almost seemed to be peeling as if from some cutaneous disease.

I'm not ashamed to say I almost fainted there and then, dear reader. That loathsome image will haunt me the rest of my days.

The next thing I heard was a loud thud from outside and below, and turning around, I found Bill nowhere to be seen. But, before I could comprehend my abandonment, the intruders seized me and pinned me down to the ground. They tied my ankles and wrists together as the most infinite terror flooded every vein in my body. I saw my pathetic, lonely, orphan life flashing before my eyes as three of the malformed creatures lifted me into the air and proceeded to carry me out of the room and into the corridor.

I felt truly resigned to my fate, and made no attempt to escape. As I was taken downstairs, the only thought present was this: Fuck Bill. Fuck Bill in his selfish fucking face.

I closed my eyes so as not to increase my torment by staring at the loathsome cultists. I cursed myself for ever agreeing to work for Bill. I cursed myself for listening to stupid ghouls in my stupid dreams. I cursed myself for ever thinking it was a good idea to spend the night in this odious town. Unadulterated shame was all I felt then — the terror had evidently reached such a maximum that, in want of reaching new heights, it had inadvertently circled back around to a minimum.

I could hear and feel that we were now outside and they were carrying me through the dreadful nightmare streets. Opening one eye a fraction, I saw that we were moving through an exceptionally narrow and dark alley where the moonbeams did not reach.

Again, I thought: Fuck Bill.

I could not believe he had abandoned me so wantonly. Then again, I could very easily believe it. I just couldn't believe that he would be the one to cost me my life.

Seconds melted into minutes, and my grip on reality loosened with every step my kidnappers took. I soon felt the seaside wind whipping at my face, and the unbelievable stench of rotting fish overwhelming my senses. I almost felt as if suffocating. I then felt my handlers awkwardly placing me down on a seat, and I couldn't help but open my eyes once again. They had placed me down within the mock steam-train I had seen from afar when first we entered this cursed town — that evident failure of a tourist attraction. I looked ahead, and saw the miniature rail stretching out along the pier towards Devil Reef. I knew then that that is where their sacrifices must have taken place.

The train presently kicked into gear and began travelling out over the sea towards that apocalyptic black rock and the repugnant building on top of it. On the train, I counted that there were, in fact, four monstrosities accompanying me – one far more degenerated than the others, and looking so far from human that I couldn't help but feel an extreme nausea at even the slightest glimpse of its deformed figure.

Below us, the tireless black sea surged and swelled with a menacing character; and looking up above, the light of the moon was diminished by thick, hateful clouds that covered the offensive sky.

Then, suddenly, the train jolted to a stop, even though we were not yet halfway to the reef. Craning my neck behind me, I made out in the distance a dark figure slowly making its way towards us from shore along the pier.

As the figure continued to approach, my heart began to quicken, and on making out the finer details of them, my heart filled with joy. It was Bill – and clenched between his bared teeth were a bunch of frayed wires. Coming to a stop near the back of the train, he spat the wires out into the wild sea and grimaced.

"No one takes my fucking Todd."

Chapter Seven.

Digging a hand into his dirty white underpants, Bill then withdrew his revolver, and with theatrical finesse, aimed it at one of the beasts.

"Hand him over and no one gets hurt," he said. Without waiting for a response, he then fired, blowing the head clean off his target. "Fine. Have it your way."

The three other cultists then howled a hideous cry in unison and scrambled their lopsided way over the train towards Bill, bloody revenge clearly on their minds. In response, Bill began brazenly firing into them, screaming as he went, "You freaky fuckers ain't laying a freaky hand on my fracking Todd!"

All previous hatred towards Bill dissipated into the ether, and I found myself cheering him on as he slaughtered the mongrels, bullets tearing through their weird, subhuman flesh. Although my view was obstructed by the train, and my movement sorely limited by my bonds, I heard two bodies hit the ground, and guttural screams ring out into the cold sea air. Such joy I felt as then cannot be expressed in words. It was as if a veil of apocalyptic doom had been lifted from my head, and a sweet angel made love to my soul. I was not to die that night.

The next sound, however, was not so pleasant – it was the sound of Bill's gun jamming. This was shortly followed by a curt "Shit." The most degraded of the bunch, being the only creature left, took foul advantage of Bill's crisis, leaping on him without hesitation.

"Bill!" I screamed as I struggled to break free of my shackles. I could see the pair of them tossing and turning over the tracks, and my heart almost leapt from my mouth as they came within an inch of the edge, within an inch of rolling over into the unknowable depths of the raging sea.

With strength I can only explain with allusions to a higher power, I burst free from my restraints and clambered desperately towards Bill in his death struggle. The demented mutant was straddling him, its thick stubby claws clamped around his stubbled neck. Without so much as a second's thought, I leapt, and tackled the beast off Bill.

"Christ, Todd," Bill gasped, clasping his neck and refilling his lungs. I held down the evil creature as it struggled to break free, gargling and writhing with unnatural loathsomeness. Bill quickly clambered to his feet and pushed me off, before punching the monstrosity in the face. "Dick."

Bill and I looked at one another and shared a small relieved smile. "Thanks for coming back for me," I said.

"Yeah, well, I felt pretty shit about leaving you to die." Bill's smile then dissipated, and his face took on an angry residue. "That doesn't mean I care about you or anything. You're still just an assistant – didn't wanna bother training a new one, is all."

"Oh."

Bill's detainee then spat on his forehead, and we were both reminded of its existence. Bill wiped off the odorous slobber as it oozed down his nose. "You bitch." He gave the creature a hard backhand across the face. "Okay, listen up. What's gonna happen now is we're gonna ask questions, and you're gonna answer them, right? Or you'll be getting one of these…" Bill picked up his revolver from the wet planks beside him and exhibited the one remaining bullet in its magazine, "in your skull. Sent at like a rapid pace so it kills you. Understand?" It was then that I saw what Bill had spent the previous night carving into his gun.

"Bill, is that a shark?"

"Yeah, d'ya like it?" Bill said proudly. "'Cos last night I was thinking – if we end up fighting these things, you know, we've gotta be prepared. Gotta have weapons that'll work against them – like with silver for werewolves. And, you know, these guys are sort of fishy, so I thought – what's a fish's weakness? Well, obviously it's a shark. They eat fish, don't they? So, I carved a shark into me gun and every bullet.

And, well, not to toot me own horn or anything, but I think it's worked *pretty* well." Bill gestured to the mutilated bodies around us.

"Right… I'm thinking maybe that was just the bullets."

Bill turned back to his interrogee, unconvinced. "So, come on, mate. Fess up. Are you a member of the Esoteric Order of Dagon?"

The creature shook its head, puzzled.

"You're not?" Bill was evidently surprised, as was I. "Remember, you better not be lying to me." He waved his revolver as a reminder. "Are you or are you not a member of the Esoteric Order of Dagon?"

The creature hesitated, then shook its head again. With much difficulty, it tried to say something. "Dong… G'no… Ward… Dawis." Given the extent of this individual's deformity, its mouth was clearly not designed for human language.

"What? What are you saying?" Bill asked.

"I think it said it doesn't know what that is," I replied.

"Is that true?" Bill said, turning back to the creature. "You've never heard of the Esoteric Order of Dagon?"

It shook its head. "Nerber."

"What the fuck?" Bill turned to me. "There's that loser husband's theory out the window then."

"If you're not working with the Esoteric Order of Dagon, who are you working with?" I asked. "What were you going to do with me?"

"Hey, I'm asking the questions here," Bill said. "You're only an assistant, remember? It's your job to watch and learn."

"Sorry."

He turned back to the creature. "If you're not working with the Esoteric Order of Dagon, who are you working with? What were you going to do with Todd?"

"Dake... Im... Do... Ar... Farder," it bungled. "We... Famiwee."

Bill whipped to me. "Translation, mate?"

I thought for a second, listening back in my mind to what I had just heard. "Take me to your father?" I asked. It nodded. "You're a family?" It nodded again.

"Your father?" Bill asked. "Who's this father? Where's this father?"

The creature wormed free one of its arms under Bill's leg and pointed towards the building on Devil Reef.

"Probably could have guessed that one." Bill appeared disappointed with himself. "And what were you gonna do with Todd? Sacrifice him?"

The creature shook its head fervently. "Nerber... No... Wee...Zave... Im... Ar... Farder... Geef... Im... Nuu... Libe."

"Give him a new life?" Bill checked. It nodded. "Not gonna lie, mate. That just sounds like you're gonna kill him."

The creature shook his head urgently again. "No...We... No... Herd... N... E... Worn."

"Well, we'll see about that." Bill then took the revolver and blew the creature's brains out.

"Bill!" I screamed.

"What? He was gonna sacrifice you. He's a fucking half-breed freak."

"He was helping us! He said he *wasn't* gonna sacrifice me."

Bill stood, wiping the steaming hot blood off the barrel of his revolver. "And you believed him?" Bill laughed to himself. "Mate, when you've been in the industry as long as me, you learn one rule – never trust no one. Or rather, always never trust anyone. Everyone's evil. Everyone's out to get ya. No one's nice." Bill's eyes dropped away from mine in what seemed a genuine effect of sadness. "You better close up that bleeding heart of yours before it gets ya killed."

I looked away from the bloody corpse and wondered to myself whether perhaps Bill was right. After all, he had been doing this forty years, and me, not even four months. Perhaps the world really was as evil as he said it was. Perhaps in this cold universe, empathy really was a weakness.

I hoped not.

When I turned back around, Bill was clumsily trying to remove the several strange golden rings from the cadaver's fingers. Finally succeeding, he pocketed them and stood up, full of glee. "Come on then," he said, marching towards Devil Reef. "We got some father to meet."

***

Pushing open a paltry door, resting half off its hinges, we entered the abandoned tourist center. It was a plain and generic room, the walls plastered with educational infographics gleaming with shiny pictures, and popping with bold colors and loud fonts. The whole effect was garish to the eye, and oddly sickening.

"Vader?" Bill called out. "Oh, vader?"

"Bill," I hissed.

"That's German for father!"

"I know, but be quiet."

"What?" he laughed. "There's no one bloody here."

He was right. There wasn't. And as Bill began inspecting the room, I too ambled my way over to the far corner and began to read one of the infographics which had in its center a crude graphic of the reef and its caves.

Have you heard the legend of old Captain Obed Marsh and his bargains with the devil?!

It has been said he and his followers performed devil worship and made human sacrifices right here on this very rock! Scary!

An old wives' tale speaks of Innsmouth folk seeing legions of devils — spawn of an ancient sea god called Dagon — emerging from caves in this rock, sprawling and dancing about this reef, before leaving wonderful jewelry as gifts for Obed Marsh.

The legend became so popular that back in the shipping days, sailors would go out of their way just to avoid coming too close to the reef! Talk about spooky!

I moved onto the next one.

In 1838, Obed Marsh founded the 'Esoteric Order of Dagon', a quasi-pagan cult imported from the East. It quickly spread and took hold of the town as a coincidental increase in the local population of fish, and subsequently the wealth of this fishing town, made the simple townsfolk believe it was all the work of this new religion.

Years later, even crazier tales began to circulate. There was talk of Obed Marsh mating with the underwater devils, creating a race of half-breed aquatic humans! Can you believe it?!

Of course, there is no scientific evidence to back up any of these claims, but that doesn't make them any less fun to consider!

"Bingo," Bill shouted, and turning around, I found him holding open a trapdoor.

"How did you find that?" I asked.

Bill tapped his nose. "A gentleman never tells."

I slowly approached it. "Where does it go?"

"God knows, but it's gotta go somewhere. Probs into some cave system or something. Probs where they do their sacrifices. Only one way to find out for sure though." Bill gestured down the steep stairs which sunk into a dense darkness. "Ladies first."

***

The narrow stairway led infinitely down like some hideous, haunted well, spiraling exhaustively. The flashlight on my phone could not light the unknown depths towards which we were heading, and if not for the time on my phone, I would have lost track of the minutes we spent descending.

"We must be leagues under the sea by now," Bill said after an uncomfortably long and tense period of silence, and I could notice a little terror in his voice I did not often hear.

"Leagues is actually a measure of horizontal distance, not vertical," I replied. "'Twenty thousand leagues under the sea' meant they travelled twenty thousand leagues *while* they were under the sea, not twenty thousand leagues *down* under the sea."

"Yeah, well, *I* meant you can shut your bloody mouth, ya nerd. No one likes a smart ass, especially one with your face."

I resolved to continue descending that awful abyssal darkness in silence.

At some point, the stairway lost its regularity and began to change wildly in direction and steepness, and after an especially shallow segment, in which we had to stoop to proceed, we suddenly emerged in a most colossal open cave.

Other than the tiny ineffective cone of light in front of us, originating from my phone, we were enveloped by a total and almost palpable blackness of the bowels of the earth. Slowly but surely, we continued on along the rocky, damp floor.

"Can you hear that?" Bill asked. Pausing, I listened. There was a strange periodic swell of what seemed like white noise, and now that my mind was paying attention, it produced in me an irrational and primal fear. "I think that's the sea above us. I think those are waves."

"I'm not going to lie, Bill," I said. "I'm really scared. I think I'm the most terrified I've ever been."

"You know what, mate? Pussy." With this, Bill took the lead and continued over the unsteady rock and shallow puddles. My mind whirled with mad thoughts of what we would uncover here, so deep below the treacherous ocean. Would we really come across a legion of devils? Perhaps we would find a horde of that alien jewelry instead. Perhaps the bodies of our contact and her husband. Perhaps their decayed son. Maybe even the corpse of old Obed Marsh.

A scutter echoing through the vacuous cavern stopped me in my tracks, and I instinctively grabbed hold of Bill in fright. When I felt his bare skin, I remembered that he was still just in his whiteys. "What was that?" I asked.

"I don't know." He readied his gun. "But if I were a betting man, which I am, I'd say another one of those fish freaks."

And then the most terrifying and utterly unfortunate of events occurred; my phone ran out of battery, and we were left in complete and total darkness. I spun around, fear disorienting both my mind and body, the abyss stretching out from us ad infinitum.

"Bill," I whimpered.

"Stop that!" he shouted back with a determined ferocity. "You're getting me scared too…"

In the darkness, my mind began to conjure cruel and gruesome images – all around us, I thought I caught glimpses of creatures similar to the most degraded of the pack who had stolen me away. Those prying bulbous eyes. That slimy blue-gray skin. That demented gait of theirs.

And then another scutter echoed around us and I had to do my very best not to relieve my bowels.

"I think we should go," I sputtered.

"What? When we're so close to finally finding out what the hell's really going on?"

"I think I can live with the mystery if it means I actually live."

"Nah, we ain't backing out now." Bill grabbed me by the arm, and marched me forward into the unknown blackness. "If you see something, give me a time and I'll shoot."

"Give you a time?" I questioned.

"Yeah, you know, like two o'clock – blam! Two thirty – blam! Two fourty-five – blam! Got a stiff shoulder so I can only really do between two and three. You should work on ya backrubs."

We continued on like this for either one minute or twenty – it is hard to remember looking back now – but finally we were gifted something that made me both sigh in relief and shake in terror: light.

It was the phosphorescent light of bioluminescent algae, swirling round and round an expansive whirlpool in aquamarine beauty, and it lay down the bottom of a gentle incline from us. The juxtaposition of this heavenly far-off sight somehow made the horrific darkness directly around us all the more terrifying.

As we approached the hypnotic glowing whirlpool, careful not to slip on any loose stones on the rocky, slippery incline, I noticed an outcropping that overhung the luminous vortex – and on it, a figure with their arms up high, silhouetted against the enchanting blue. Getting closer, it became apparent that the figure was sitting in a chair that sparkled and gleamed with reflections of the pool, and also too, that this must have been the leader of the whole conspiracy in one way or another. The air around them seemed distorted with authority and power, and half of me wished to turn and flee at once.

Muttered incantations wafted their way up from the man in a voice both gruff and strangely familiar. I could not make out the individual words, for they were in a language I did not understand – one that seemed to bear some similarity to the ungodly croaks and belches of the deformed Innsmouth folk – but in their entirety, they appeared to be plainly sinister. And as I listened, I suddenly noticed the playing of distant pan flutes too, and I wondered when they had begun their ethereal melodies. From where this music was coming from, I could not say. It seemed from everywhere and nowhere all at once.

Now only a dozen yards or so from the man, we halted in our approach, and looking up at him on his rocky outcropping, he seemed to sense our presence. He dropped his arms, ceased his incantations, and turned his golden gem-encrusted wheelchair around to face us.

Bill slowly cocked his revolver and aimed it at the mysterious fellow. We held our breaths.

"My children," the man said in a voice now uncannily familiar. "At last. The ritual has been prepared." The voice was worn out, gravelly, and extremely Australian – in short, it was Bill's. And as the man turned, I saw his fingers comprehensively covered with that peculiar golden jewelry, thick with gems and stones of old. And round his neck lay strange embraided golden chains so heavy that his head seemed almost weighed down by their presence, and in his ears, jewels so excessive and rich in color that I almost missed the most surprising feature of all – for where the man's eyes should have been, there were only dark sunken holes.

And almost choking on his words, with bewilderment and reverence, Bill called out, "Dad?"

Chapter Eight.

"Bill?" Bruce answered. (His name was Bruce, by the way, as I would later come to learn.) "Is that you?"

"Yeah, Dad, it's me..." Bill shone with a boy-like wonder, and in that moment even the air seemed to hold its breath. I felt gravity weaken its grip as if momentarily forgetting its purpose, drawn into the scene by a curiosity it had not felt in aeons, and we all appeared to imperceptibly float with the momentousness of this magical reunion of father and son.

"What the bloody hell are you doing here?" Bruce snapped. His voice projected a deep irritation far beyond any mortal comprehension.

"That's the first thing you say to me after forty years?" There was an impeccable crack in Bill's voice, and I saw his whole demeanor shrink with these words. "And what's up with the weird holes where your eyes should be?"

"Answer my bloody question, ya bogan — what the shit are you doing here?"

"You ain't got no eyes, Dad. And you're in a wheelchair. And you're living in a fucking cave. What's happened to you?"

"What. Are. You. Doing here?"

"Well, to be perfectly honest, Dad," Bill replied, crossing his arms. "Investigating your bodgie cult, apparently. You're the one they're calling 'Our Father', I presume?"

"Ah, so you've met your halfsiblings then. I do hope you played nice."

"My halfsiblings?" At this frightful revelation, I saw Bill swallow and turn several shades paler. "Right, well, yeah, you know... shot them to shit-shit-the shit. Shot the shit. With them." Bill steadied himself by grabbing hold of his hips. "So, they're me brothers and sisters, yeah? Me actual brothers and sisters? They're your actual kids?" Bill looked as if he were mere moments away from regurgitating yesterday's McDonalds.

"They are mine and Dagon's offspring, yes."

"Dagon!" I could not help but exclaim.

"What!" Bill chimed in. "Dagon! What the fuck? What the actual fuck?"

"Isn't Dagon an old god?" I asked.

"Young enough for me," Bruce replied.

"What? Just what? Just what?" Bill turned away from his father and began pacing up and down as if searching for an answer to all this newfound madness. Coming up empty handed, he spun back around with an accusing finger. "You mean you slept with the enemy? You just went ahead and went against everything you used to stand for? Against all your life's work? *Our* life's work? You just decided to fuck it?"

Bruce unfurled a mischievous smile. "Oh, come on, Bill. Don't tell me you've never been tempted."

I turned to Bill and saw in his eyes a betrayal of guilt and shame. "Nah... dunno what you're on about. Literally no idea what you're on about." Bill caught eye contact with me and instantly looked away. "How does that even work anyway? You and Dagon? You and an old god? Do they even have a sex? What are the mechanics?"

"You don't want to know," he replied gravely.

"Who's the one getting pregnant?"

"You don't. Want. To know."

Bill turned away from his father, rubbing his forehead in earnest stress. "Dad. I'm really seriously confused right now. Like, me brain's going right troppo. I have so many questions."

"And I don't have any answers for you, so why don't you see yourself out the way you came in. And don't bother coming back again." After a grave and pregnant pause, he continued with sadistic glee, "You know, I'd almost forgotten how much I despised being in your presence. Your pathetic, pitiful presence. My life has been so much happier since I left you all those years ago."

"Don't you think *I* deserve some answers?" I bravely interrupted, stepping forward, feeling oddly protective over Bill. The mystery of the whole situation was also weighing heavy on my tired mind. "I was kidnapped by your children. Yours and Dagon's children. What were they going to do with me?"

"Sorry, but who the fuck are you?" Bruce replied with a uniquely hurtful antipathy.

"He's my friendsistant, Dad." Bill stepped forward and put his arm around me. "And he's right. He deserves answers – as do I. Just what the hell is going on here? And what happened to your fucking eyes?"

"Bill," Bruce replied curtly, his face contorting with omens of violent intent, his sunken holes squirming with glee. "My darling boy. I'm only going to say this one more time. Leave. Right now. And never come back."

After a few seconds of taut stillness, the corner of Bill's mouth began to curl. "I see what you're doing." He chuckled, waving his finger like Sherlock Holmes as it all came together in his mind. "I see…" He guffawed to himself boastfully.

"What are you on about, you half-witted mongrel?" Bruce's voice contained an ancient fatigue.

"Reverse psychology. I see right through you, ol' man." Bill's laughter grew several degrees more insane and maniacal. "Ha ha ha, I nearly fell for it too! Jesus, how could I have been so stupid! You want me to join your cult, don't you? Jesus Christ, it's so obvious now. You wanted to see me beg to join ya cult, didn't you? You wanted the satisfaction of seeing me beg before agreeing to take me in and working as partners again. You're probably the one who called me round to investigate too, aren't ya? There is no old woman and her missing husband. Ha ha ha, I see it now! I see it all. And Jesus, what a pathetic plan." Bill spat on the ground. "Guess what, Dad? It's not happening. Not happening in a million years! I'll never join your sick cult no matter how much you want me to – that's just not me."

"Bill. Let me be perfectly, unambiguously, categorically clear." With each word, Bruce grew louder and more enraged. "I do not want – and never will want – you to be a member of this family. AM I CLEAR?"

"Yeah, you do," Bill shot back.

"No, I don't."

"Not even a little bit?"

"No!"

"Please."

"NO!"

"That's it. You've gone fully bonkers, Dad. I'm getting you outta here. This seaside air's rotting ya brain." Bill marched forward with no trace of trepidation. "Come on, time to go. Time to come home."

"Don't you lay a fucking finger on me," Bruce barked back, but ignoring him, Bill scooped up the crippled man and slung him over his shoulder. His chains and rings clattered like dull chimes. "Come on, Todd. Let's go."

"Put me DOWN!" Suddenly, the scuttering that had greeted us on first arrival to this cave returned –

though multiplied a hundredfold – from all around us, above and below.

"Bill… Are you sure we should be doing this?"

"He's me Dad, Todd. I can't just leave him here, can I?"

"Yes, you can, you fucking idiot, Bill. Put me down, boy! Put me down!" And lifting up his head, Bruce bellowed, "CHILDREN!"

A disgusting symphony of guttural croaks and groans and bleats and cries echoed back, transmuting my legs to jelly. I could see none of the abominable creatures, which only served to enhance the terror, but from what I was hearing, I estimated there to be thousands.

"Run!" Bill screamed as we both turned away from the glowing maelstrom and began to barrel over the rocky, uneven, slippery ground in oppressive darkness that squeezed and pushed with a spiteful vengeance.

"TAKE THEM!" Bruce roared. His words were textured with an absolute authority, and at once, the scuttering and muttering amplified to earthshattering magnitudes. Bill was surprisingly quick for a middle-aged man carrying an old man, complete with a shop's worth of jewelry, and it was all I could do to keep up with them without losing my footing and falling to the ground and most probably my doom.

"What happened to your eyes, Dad?" Bill yelled over the blind chaos. "Just tell me, what happened to your fucking eyes?"

"I think that can wait, Bill!" I yelled back.

"Put me DOWN!"

The following sequence was so terrifying and so absolutely beyond anything I had ever experienced that I do not know how much of my recollection is true and how much is my mind's wild fancy, filling in blanks from memories too deranged to ever recall, but I shall write down here as much of the truth as I can retrieve from my battered psyche.

As we approached the winding staircase we had entered the cave by, I felt slippery hands grasp at my ankles, and almost fainted from shock, but my body's flight instinct was too strong to be overcome and it kept on running, lapping at Bill's tail. The endless swarm of monsters behind us, and the unadulterated terror I now felt, made the earlier hotel abduction seem like mere child's play in retrospect.

"I despise you, Bill," Bruce's strained voice screamed in Bill's ear. "Can I be any bloody clearer? I *despise* you. LEAVE ME HERE!"

"You're under Dagon's control," Bill smarmily replied as he began leaping up the spiral staircase with an agility that should have been impossible for an Olympic athlete let alone a slightly podgy Aussie. "That's what it is – mind control. That explains why you left me as a little kid. That explains why you don't want me back. That explains how you went from a hero exterminating cosmic threats to a villain sleeping with them!"

"Stop this, Bill! This is embarrassing. Just embarrassing."

I did not want to look back, but I could hear the hordes of fiends scrambling their way over one another to ascend the narrow and steep stairway and bring us to our knees. In my mind, I imagined their horrific bulbous eyes, their disgusting shiny skin, and their beastly hopping manner of locomotion.

"You're clearly jealous," Bruce continued. "You've always been a jealous one – it's one of the many reasons I never liked you."

"Jealous?" Bill laughed. "Me? Jealous? Me? Jealous?"

"Yes."

"Jealous of fish freaks who murder people?"

Despite all the pandemonium, I could not help but find myself impressed at Bill's ability to continue a conversation whilst running for his life up a flight of stairs *and* carrying his conversation-partner.

"No!" Bruce barked back, and in a peculiarly clear and loud manner, he carefully added, "We DO NOT murder people. We give them a NEW LIFE."

"Whatever," Bill grumbled, unconvinced. "I'm not jealous. I'm just your son – and I'm saving you."

In a whirlwind of nightmares, we finally emerged out of the spiraling stairway and into the tourist center. As soon as I was out of the stairway, Bill threw the trapdoor shut, and shoved me down on top of it. "Now, stay there and keep it closed while I go get the van."

"What?" I could already feel several prying hands pushing up against the flap, scratching at the wood and trying to rip it open. "I'm not staying here."

"You'll be fine," Bill said, heading to the door before crying out in pain. I then noticed that Bruce had his yellowed, sharpened teeth sunk deep into Bill's shoulder.

"Lemmego," Bruce moaned with his mouth full. "Yurnotsavinme, yurkidnappinme."

The trapdoor rattled and shook with Bill's halfsiblings' increasingly desperate attempts to break free. Bill, however, was not paying attention to me or his pursuers, rather he was busy trying to pry his father's jaw open. "I *am* saving you," he said. "You've gone mental. You've got no eyes. You're saying you don't want nothing to do with me. You've gone completely bloody mental."

His teeth now out of Bill's shoulder, Bruce replied, "You're the mental one, you loon. Why can't ya just leave me and my new family in peace? Are ya that much of a baby?"

Bill struggled to form a response as the trap door burst open, sending me flying across the room. I scrambled to my feet as the hideous forms of those demented creatures began to swarm out of the hole like sewage out of an overflowing gutter.

"Nice work, Todd," Bill sarcastically commented before sprinting out of the center and along the pier towards shore. Chasing after him, I looked out at the moonlit town and its maze of shadow-blighted alleys. The ancient spires and roofs of decaying Innsmouth gleamed in the yellow moonlight, giving it a sickly complexion, and I was suddenly struck by the thought of how it must have looked in the old days before any of this unpleasantness had ever occurred. Or perhaps that magical, pure town of forgotten history had never really existed; perhaps that was a mere romantic fantasy of my own devising; perhaps it had always been this way – an evil of some form always in the shadows.

But this was no time for baseless conjecture – the pitter patter of wet flesh and clubbed feet on wood was seconds behind us as we scrambled round the side of the miniature train.

"So," Bill began with an incongruous nonchalance, "are ya ever gonna tell me what happened to your eyes or not?"

"Jesus Christ," Bruce replied, exasperated. "Will you put me down if I do?"

"Sure," Bill said, continuing to sprint at full pace towards Innsmouth.

"Fine then. Dagon took them from me so that I might see better."

"What?" Bill yelled. "See better? With no eyes? What are you on?"

"It was Dagon's wedding gift to me."

"What?" Bill yelled again. "You remarried? Where was my invite? And what sort of a wedding gift is that? I know I'm not one to talk, Dad, but that don't sound like a healthy relationship to me. A normal present is… I dunno, a Wii fit. Or a—"

"Put me down now! I've told you now so put me down!"

"Soz, Dad, I was telling a porky. I ain't leaving you for nothing."

It was when I glanced behind me and saw the most horrible impression of all – that of an undulating limitless stream of hundreds of those foul beasts, both on the tracks and in the sea, the moonlit waters of which were squirming alive with a teeming horde of incomprehensible shapes and terrors – that I continued to question whether Bill was taking the right course of action. My mind could not help but stir with visions of tripping up Bill and letting the wicked devils have their father back. Although I cared for Bill, I was not prepared to sacrifice my own life just for him to have a chance of 'rescuing' his unwilling and thoroughly unpleasant father.

We made our way off the pier and into town as Bill tried to recall what the quickest way back to the hotel was, the parking lot of which our van was still in. "Left," I shouted as I saw Bill snapping his head around in a wild frenzy.

"Cheers, mate," he shouted back.

Lucky for us, it appeared as if the deformed creatures chasing us did not have bodies built for speed on land, and so, on the terrifying and dark sprint back to the hotel, we managed to put quite a buffer between us and our pursuers.

However, on entering the parking lot, we were struck with a most heart-wrenching and stomach-knotting sight. Our van no longer had any tires.

Bill skidded to a stop. "Oh, fuck me. Fucking fuck me."

"Bill, just give him back," I pleaded. "Give him back or we're not making it out of this town alive."

"Your friendsistant's right, Bill. If you let me go now, I'll let you leave this town unharmed. If not, you shall both suffer a most violent death. And I think that's very fair seeing as how you already killed some of me kids."

Bill shot him a guilty look.

"Yeah, that's right – I saw their corpses on the pier. You're caught."

"I'm not giving you back!" Bill screamed before gargling vehemently. He then spun to me with a wild conviction. "Todd, think. Where can we go that's safe? Where can we go to wait this out?"

***

Under the shining golden arches, Bill kicked in the front door and headed for the counter. "We'll hide in the freezer and interrogate me dad in there. Find out what's really going on. Give him a bit of the old ice torture if needs be."

"You will do nothing of the bloody sort," Bruce barked back, still struggling to break free with the lackluster aid of his powerless legs.

"Do you think they followed us?" Bill asked as I peered out the windows.

"I can't see them."

"Good. Over here then." He then threw his dad over the counter, adding an "Oops."

"You bloody daglock," the old man croaked, rubbing his bruised head as Bill hopped over and picked him back up.

"Maybe you should start treating me a bit nicer then, eh?" Bill tried to open the freezer-room but found it locked. "Todd, find the keys."

"It's pretty dark," I replied.

"Oh right. Weird. I don't remember asking if it was dark. Did I ask if it was dark, Dad? No, I don't think I did. I think I said find the fucking keys!"

Bill was clearly in a state of severe irritation, and given the pressure of the situation, I felt it best not to argue. I got to work, and prayed the beasts didn't find us.

Chapter Nine.

Inside the damnably frosty freezer-room, Bill stood above his father who laid helpless on the floor, one foot either side of his limp, withered legs.

"I'm done messing around," Bill said. "You're gonna answer me straight now, you hear?"

"Who the hell do you think you are? John bloody Wayne? Go to hell, you damn bogan."

Bill looked at me and nodded, and as previously agreed, I grabbed ahold of Bruce's hand and pulled a malformed golden ring off of one of his fingers. "You bitch! Give that back." I handed it to Bill who placed the ring proudly on one of his own fingers.

"For every evasion or lie, you lose one of your precious blood rings," Bill taunted. "That's the only thing you really care about, isn't it? Gold. That's the only thing that's gonna get a reaction out of you."

"When Dagon gets their hands on you..." Bruce chuckled psychotically. "You're going to join me in wishing you were never born."

Bill looked at me and nodded again, and fighting off Bruce's weak attempts at defiance, I took another of his alien golden rings and handed it to Bill. "That goes for threats too." Bruce cried and stretched out his hands like a baby for its pacifier. "First question – are you running a cult? More specifically, are you behind the return of the Esoteric Order of Dagon?"

"No!"

"And that's a lie, so say bye-bye – to one of ya rings." I took another and once again handed it to Bill. It fit him like a glove.

"Why are ya asking me questions if you think you already know the answers, ya friggen moron?"

"To see if you're prepared to look your own son in the eye and lie to his face – and now I know you are, so… I'm sad."

"I'm not lying." The old man sighed contemptuously. "I'm not running a cult. Cults don't work no more – they've got too bad a rep. No one in their right mind would join one in this day and age. You know that as well as I do." Bill shrugged in a half-acknowledgment. "We're just a family business. Me and me kids. We do work, and we get rewarded. There's no mysticism to it, and there's no recruiting outsiders. So no, I'm not running a cult. And no, the fucking Esoteric Order of Dagon ain't returned. It's just me and me kids, alright? Well, me and the ones I actually like."

Bill mused for a while. "Alright, you can keep a ring for that. You weren't completely honest – more like politician-honest – but that's better than nothing.

Next question, what's this 'work' you're supposedly doing? One of your kids, one of my… brothers… said you're givin' people you kidnap a new life – that's bullshit, isn't it?"

"Of course it's bullshit," Bruce groaned. "But kids today are so squeamish. They don't wanna hear that all they're really doing is just some good old sacrificing of souls in return for material rewards, ya know? Although they probably know in the back of their minds that that's what's really going on, they don't wanna hear it outright. So, I wrap it up in a little fairytale story of giving people a new life, give them their gold, and send them on their happy, unquestioning way. Bunch a friggen babies, the lot of 'em."

"And who are you sacrificing the townsfolk to? Dagon?"

"Enough with the fucking questions!" Bruce yelled, shaking free of my grip. "And give me my bloody rings back! Yes, Dagon and the Deep Ones. Yes, that's who we're sacrificing to. Yes, that's who's giving us the jewelry. Who gives a shit? It's just another business. It's all the same. Now let me go!" Growling, he locked eyes with Bill. "Give me my rings back, get the hell out of here, and I won't set the dogs on you. Alright? We'll call it quits, water under the bridge, and go our separate ways. I think that'd be best for everyone, don't you? So, how about it? Do we have a deal, son?"

Bill looked at me with searching eyes. "Do it," I quietly answered. "We've got our answers now. Give him his rings back and let's go." I saw indecision in Bill's eyes – a longing for a world that didn't exist and a reluctance to accept the one that did. But looking sorrowfully down, he began taking off his newly acquired trinkets.

"I'm not happy about this, Dad."

"Neither am I," he replied. "I never wanted you to find me. I knew you'd cause a scene."

And handing back the rings, Bill watched Bruce slide them on with glee. "Thank you, Bill. Thank you. Now, for my end of the bargain." An evil grin spread across his face like wildfire. "CHILDREN! CHILDREN! I'M IN MICKEY D'S! SAVE ME! SAVE ME!"

Bill leapt on his father, who curled up into a ball to protect his bejeweled hands. "You fucker!" Bill looked to his side, and seeing a bag full of frozen fries, ripped a hole in its side and grabbed a handful. Forming a misshapen dagger out of the frozen potato product, he plunged it deep into one of Bruce's recessed eyeholes, twisting it as if stubbing out a cigarette. Bruce screamed in unimaginable pain. "You lying fuckeroon! You abominable shit!" He then pulled back, throwing the fries aside. "I've changed me mind – you're clearly still under Dagon's mind control. I'm getting you out of here. I'm rescuing you."

"Bill, no!" I yelled.

"There's no rescuing me," Bruce replied through shallow, pained breaths. "When Dagon awakes at daybreak and finds me gone, they'll get me back whatever it costs – because they love me, and they *need* me. Something you'll never understand."

Bill laughed. "What the hell could an Old God need you for?"

"You'll see." Bruce began hysterically cackling. "Soon, you'll see!"

Just then, we all heard the front door of the McDonalds bang open. "Children!" Bruce called out. "Children, save me!"

A series of croaking, baying voices replied, which would have sent chills up my spine if not for the fact that we were already in a freezer. Bill stood up and readied his revolver. "Remember this, Dad?" he said, brandishing the weapon proudly. "This was your revolver. Now, I'm going to use it to kill your chimera kids." Bill swung open the door and stepped out, and from within the confines of the freezer-room, through the open doorway, I saw him raising the revolver and cocking it.

"Bill, just let him go," I cried. "It's not worth it. Let's just get out of here." But Bill was in a world of his own and my cries went unheard.

"Come on, ya sprogs," Bill bellowed. "Come fight the OG. You motherfroggers ain't got nothing on me." His siblings croaked and squealed back in aggressive defiance, but Bill just grinned and pulled the trigger.

And the gun jammed.

Bill spun his head to me, a feral panic in his eyes, then a leaping blur flew towards him and sent him tumbling down the corridor, out of my sight. A ripping and biting of flesh echoed out as Bill's primordial screams joined them in a symphony of true terror. At this, Bruce cackled violently.

I rushed out of the freezer and turned the corner to see two of the monsters sat atop Bill, clawing at his face as he hysterically attempted to push them off. I turned and rushed into the kitchen to find a knife, but after a brief scan, the closest implement to a weapon I could find was a small spatula. Given the time restraints of the situation, however, I determined that I would have to make do with the tools at hand (even if it did have no shark carved into it).

I grabbed the spatula and rushed back to Bill and his attackers. With all the strength I could muster I began spanking the hideous creatures, and thankfully, this seemed to be enough of a distraction for Bill to gain the upper hand and break free of their hold. Emerging from under them, however, and to my horror, I noticed that one of his eyes was now totally bloody and mangled. In fact, upon scrutinizing the wound further, I came to the realization that there was no eye left at all – it had been gorged out – and as one of the creatures turned to attack me, this prognosis was confirmed by an eye stem dangling out of its deformed mouth. A wave of rage overwhelmed me and I began to relentlessly bludgeon the sick brute in the face.

Bill, I noticed, had turned his revolver around and was now using it as a primitive club to batter the attackers too. "You bitches. You little bitches," he cried out in savage agony. Before I was able to catch a breath, the monsters were lying on the floor, twitching, and clearly no longer a threat.

"We need to get the fuck out of here," Bill said. "And quick."

"Bill, what in the actual fuck? Your fucking eye."

"What about it?"

"What do you mean? It's been torn out. You're missing a fucking eye."

"No, I'm not."

"What are you on about? We need to stop this. Now."

"I'm not giving him back. He's me dad."

"He doesn't even like you. Why are you doing this? You've already lost an eye. Like, a whole eye. What next? Your legs?"

"I'm telling you, I ain't lost no eye. It's just shut."

"What?"

"Just keeping it shut," he said, storming past me and back into the freezer-room. "Sick of depth perception." He then hoisted his protesting father back onto his shoulder and marched towards the front door.

"Bill," I began.

"Pick up a few packs of sweet and sour sauce on your way out, mate," he called back to me. "Love that shit."

***

"Dagon will not let me leave," Bruce taunted as we trekked through the woods, up and out of Innsmouth. "I'm too important."

"You're kiddin' yourself if you think you're actually important to Dagon. I mean, they're a fuckin' Old God. Can't you see? They're just using and abusing you till ya spent, then they'll move onto the next willing incubator. Anyway, we'll be long gone before Dagon finds you missing."

Looking at the coastline, I saw the horizon slowly brightening. "Looks like it's nearly sunrise now actually, Bill," I said. Bruce had kindly informed us at the beginning of our ascent that every sunrise, on the dot, Dagon and he made love. Or rather, whatever you'd call something that leads to those deformed Innsmouth folk. He said not once in thirty years had he ever missed it.

"Alright," Bill replied, spinning around. "Fuck sake – guess we're gonna have to go with plan B then."

"There's a plan B?"

"Todd, you take Dad's clothes, go back to the reef, get in the wheelchair, put on an Aussie accent, and pretend to be the ol' man. That should buy me and Dad enough time to get out of here. Then, I dunno, in a couple months or whatever, you can escape and come find us."

"What?" I said, trying not to pay too much attention to Bill's gruesome optical wound, fighting my eyes' morbid curiosity to see what had become of their own kind. "What sort of a plan is that? That's not gonna work."

"He's right," Bruce agreed. "Dagon knows every inch of my body."

"It might work long enough for us to escape — that's all we need."

"Every crevice," Bruce added.

"But what about me?" I said.

Bill shrugged. "Dunno. Don't care."

"Inside and out."

"You don't care?"

"Nah."

"Jesus Christ," I said, a sliver of reality beginning to seep back into the nightmare I was living through. "What am I doing? What the hell am I doing risking my life to save you? You're fucking mental. *I'm* fucking mental."

"I agree with the last part," Bill replied. "You'd be mental not to go along with me brilliant plan."

"You really don't care if I die or not, do you? You're a psychopath. You're an actual psychopath. This is what happened to your last assistant too, isn't it? Jackie." At this accusation, Bill's face deformed and twisted with elemental disgust. Feeling I was touching a nerve, I pressed on, wishing to twist the knife. "She was the woman in your painting, wasn't she? Why were you painting her? To exorcise your guilt? To bring her back to life? You killed her with one of your selfish half-baked fucking plans, didn't you? That's what happened. And that's what's going to happen to me."

Bill dropped his father onto the damp ground and marched towards me till his nose was touching mine. "How bleeping dare you," he spat. "You've got no clue what the hell you're talking about."

"Tell me then. What happened to her? What did I see in my dream? What…" I looked him up and down, lost for words, then brought out my phone. Turning it around, I showed him the reflection of his own gouged out eye in the black mirror of its dead screen. "What made you this?"

Just then, the sun peeked over the horizon, flooding the forest with a thick, orange haze, catching all our attentions. Bruce began cackling on the floor. "Dagon!" he cried out. "Oh, Dagon! Dagon! Dagon!"

And in the far distance of the ocean, I saw waves make way for something colossal moving under the surface, and in my bones I felt a shifting of energy in the air as if a great magnet was slowly emerging from another dimension. And up through the ancient waters of deepest mysteries, the head of a spectral unearthly creature, of size even now I cannot comprehend, surfaced – and with it, an ungodly cry of such pitch and volume that on cold nights I can still hear it ringing through my head.

Instantly, I was struck by unreality and blacked out.

***

I know I've said this before but I hope that doesn't take away from the magnitude of the moment when I say that what I am about to tell you was so insanely incomprehensible, so maddeningly indecipherable, that mere letters arranged in simple (or even complex) words will never do the experience even a minuscule modicum of justice.

On an onyx pavement that stretched into infinity, I suddenly found myself walking. I do not remember how I got there or even awakening in this strange situation – it was as if I had always been walking, and I was merely realizing it for the first time. Either side of this modest path were windy meadows complete with scented grasses and brilliant flowers, and approaching up ahead looked an onyx crossroads of sorts, eight paths in total. It was when turning my attention to the figures I then saw walking along the other pavements that I was struck by an existential terror and dread so complete that I had never before thought it possible feelings could be felt so viscerally and with such totality.

For it was I on those other pavements – all I. Perfect copies on each and every one of the eight paths, and all inspecting one another just as I was. Perhaps I was them. Or perhaps they were me. Or perhaps we were all mere copies of another, truer Todd. Whatever the case, we all continued walking until meeting in the middle. We lifted our hands and placed each of our palms upon one another's forming a rudimentary circle of Todd flesh.

"What—?" we all began. "Who—?" we futilely continued. "Idiot," we all concluded.

Then suddenly from above, emerged an orb of glossy texture and almost impossible-to-describe color – in fact, one could only call it color by analogy, so strange and inhuman were its shifting hues. We all stared at it for what felt like a dozen eternities before it announced, in a voice that generated itself within our brains, as if vibrations in the air were too rudimentary a form of communication, "YOU ARE NOT SUPPOSED TO BE HERE."

It repeated, with perfect monotonous volume and speed, "YOU ARE NOT SUPPOSED TO BE HERE. YOU ARE NOT SUPPOSED TO BE HERE. YOU ARE NOT SUPPOSED TO BE HERE. YOU ARE NOT SUPPOSED TO BE HERE. YOU ARE NOT SUPPOSED TO BE HERE."

And just like that, I was not there. Just like that, I was standing in the middle of a slimy expanse of hellish black mire which extended about me in repetitious undulations as far as the eye could see. And it was only me – just the one me. Alone.

On the one hand, I was glad to be free of my unnerving doubles, but on the other, it seemed merely as if the quality of perfect terror had changed, not the quantity, and I trembled at the thought of what awaited me next.

In the air and rotting soil there was a sinister tone that chilled me to the very core. The region was putrid with the carcasses of decaying fish, and of other less describable things which I saw protruding from the nasty mud of the unending plain. Again, I reiterate that it is the most foolish of endeavors to even attempt to convey a modicum of the unutterable hideousness that can dwell in absolute silence and barren immensity, but again, I find myself pursuing that ineffable goal nonetheless. I am a stubborn fool.

There was nothing within hearing, and nothing within sight, save a vast reach of black slime; yet the absoluteness of the stillness and the homogeneity of the landscape oppressed me with a nauseating fear. The sun was blazing down from a sky which seemed to me almost black in its cloudless cruelty, as though reflecting the inky marsh beneath my feet.

I searched my limited brain for an explanation as to where I was and what I was seeing but could find none, other than the notion that the unhallowed scream of that infernal god must have transported my spirit to a malevolent dream world – perhaps one of its own dreaming.

After my inert osmosis of the environment, I determined to march forth, if not for morbid curiosity, then for the faint, faint hope of finding Bill somewhere in this dark realm. The soil was dry enough to walk upon with ease, but the odor of the fish was maddening and only became more so the more I walked. I walked for hours and hours with no suggestion of a change of scenery from the horizon, and soon found that even the sun had abandoned me. With the sun's disappearance, I felt weary, and saw no other option but to sit in the foul-smelling filth and try to rest. The waning gibbous moon was glowing bright, and seemed larger than on Earth, and after studying its luminous form for a time impossible to say, I imperceptibly found myself lulled to sleep by its imperfect beauty.

And in that dream within a dream, I found myself stood on the edge of a vast canyon, orange and dusty and cold to the touch. The valley went down unknown depths into evanescent darkness, and down those dizzying miles of air, spiked crags and sharp rocks jutted out from the cliff-faces like the open jaws of a behemothic shark. Presently, the desert sun eclipsed in a flash of lightning and thunder, and the landscape and I were plunged into frozen night.

With this meteoric change in atmosphere, I looked across the valley and saw another figure – this time not my own – crawling along the ground. Another flash of lightning illuminated the alien presence just long enough for me to recognize it as none other than the body of wicked Bruce. Though this comforted me somewhat, as at last I was not alone, this newfound comfort did not last long. Looking up at the clouded sky, I caught the terrible outline of something noxiously thin and horned and tailed and bat-winged. Other things too had begun to blot out patches of the dark sky as if a flock of vague entities were flapping thickly and silently, and approaching fast.

It was then that I remembered that dream, when first I had met Pickman and he had given me that drink; when first I had seen Bill and the slick, oily black demons that were holding him back – they and the ominous figures approaching me from the sky were one in the same!

Across the valley, I heard Bruce cry in terror as the faceless, silent creatures grabbed hold of his limbs, but soon the terror was far from abstract when I felt a cold rubbery hand seize my own neck. This assault was quickly followed by another frigid claw on my right foot, and yet another on my left. I cried out in horror.

And then, from out of the valley, rising on a phosphorescent cloud, was cycloptic Bill, one hand stretched up to the tempestuous heavens. And bellowing out, like a god of thunder, a lightning bolt struck his outstretched hand, materializing in it forthwith a pristine violin. And I saw him look from left to right, from me to his father, and I saw him do it again and again as the silent demons began to lift off the ground with me in their grasp.

"Bill!" Bruce called out in a voice of genuine distress and horror as he became airborne like myself.

"Bill!" I called out too, in futile hope that he might choose to save me over his somehow-beloved father.

Bill's head continued turning back and forth between his two companions on either side of the crevice, his radiant cloud gently floating on the turbulent winds, his ethereal violin at the ready. "Bill, save me, boy! Save me!" Bruce yelled as the jet-black devils took him ever higher into the stormy sky. "I'll let you join the family, son. This was all a test! You've passed! I'll let you join the family! Dear God, Bill! Please! I've always loved you! You know that! We're father and son! Save your dear Pa!"

Then, the most inexplicable thing happened – the thing that despite all I have seen, still remains to me the most cosmically incomprehensible – Bill turned his cloud to me, and flew. With his violin up high, he began to play that unearthly, cacophonous music I had heard him practicing at home, though with more vigor and manic energy than ever before. Contradictory notes and tones cut through the swirling air, and immeasurable rhythms pulsed between the falling drops of rain. This playing, perhaps coherent in another dimension or scheme of choral geometry far beyond human comprehension, on reaching whatever auditory organs these soundless nightmares had, disturbed them so much that half let loose their grip on me, and the other half seemed to spasm in disgust or revolt. With glee, I dangled high above the dusty canyon floor, fully contented with the knowledge that even if I died here, I would die knowing that Bill chose me.

He chose me.

Todd.

Upside down, I caught a final glimpse of Bruce being dragged into the murky, overcast sea of clouds below, before disappearing through them into unknown horrors. As Bill continued his manic, wild, hyperphysical playing, I felt the cold, damp grasps of obscene claws drop away in succession until only one was left. Despite the offensive sounds bursting forth from Bill's violin, this one brave warrior would not let go of its catch, and I noticed that I was once again on the rise. This load of fresh terror was lightened, however, by Bill's own ascent on his enchanted cloud as he pushed through all limits of logic to bring his playing to unfathomable heights of intensity and cryptic power.

With a screech, the creature relented and dropped me into the open air, and as I screamed, plummeting promptly to my doom, I noticed a perverse twist in Bill's music, and then I was gone.

Chapter Ten.

When I awoke, I was back on that hilltop, overlooking Innsmouth as it glimmered in the amber rays of the rising sun. Looking around, I saw Bill coming to his senses beside me. I found no trace of Bruce.

I stammered, struggling with my soul on its return to true reality (or at least what I hope to the Outer Gods is true reality). "What just happened? What was that?"

Bill shrugged, then cast his gaze around him, presumably looking for Bruce.

"I think he's gone," I said. "I don't know where, but he's gone."

Bill sat in contemplative silence for a second or two before throwing out another casual shrug. "Fair dinkums – maybe Dagon took the old bugger back. Who cares?" He then jumped to his feet, and grabbing hold of his revolver by the barrel, stretched back his arm and launched the weapon down the hill towards the town. "Holy shit! D'ya see that throw? That's gotta be, like, what? A kilometer probably. Maybe more. Crikey!"

I got to my feet and steadied myself against a tree, trying to push through the dizzying residue of our early morning foray. "Where did that scream send us?" I asked.

Bill's reply was simply another shrug.

"And those creatures… You've dealt with them before, haven't you? With Jackie. That's why you practice your violin every night, isn't it?" I studied Bill's face closely for any clue as to his past but he just looked away and rubbed his nose.

"Dunno what you're on about it."

Not wishing to let bad memories linger any longer than necessary, I merely added a humble "Thank you."

"For what?" Bill mumbled, furrowing his brow.

"You know, for… saving me," I replied. "Choosing me. I know that must have been tough."

"Dunno what you're on about, mate." Bill spun around and began marching up the hill, away from Innsmouth.

"What do you mean?" I jogged to catch up with him as fast as my tired legs would allow. "Just now. In the dream. On your cloud – with your violin – you saved me from those demon things. You chose me over your dad."

Bill waved his hand dismissively. "You're talking bollocks, mate. Must've hallucinated. You're saying I picked your sorry assistant ass over me dad? Fat chance."

Feeling there was little progress to be made down this line of questioning, I shifted gear. "But wait? What are we doing now? Just leaving? Is that it?"

"Yeah, well, the job's done, ain't it? That woman and her man got sacrificed – probably – we ain't getting no money off them, and there's nothing more we can do. So, that's it."

"But…" I began. "But that can't be it. What did we even accomplish here?"

"Well, aside from a bit of light fratricide, not too sure." Bill huffed, continuing in his single-minded march. "But that's alright. Life ain't all about accomplishing things, or understanding nothing, it's just about getting through it – and we got through it, didn't we? Ain't that enough?"

"But… But the cult's still operating. And your dad's probably just gone back to continue getting… well, whatever Dagon does with him."

"Maybe. But I'm tired. And, to be honest, I think solving this one's beyond us, Todd. We survived, and we sort of got the gist of what was going on – that's enough for me. With Dagon on their side it's just too big a problem for two blokes to handle on their own. Well, one bloke and one boy. Even if Dad didn't go back, Dagon would probably just find another poor bugger to bugger. Yep. You gotta know when to hold 'em and know when to fold 'em. And this time, I'm afraid, we gotta fold. This is a problem for higher powers than us to come and solve – it's a shame but it is what it is."

"But…" I stammered, still dissatisfied.

"We survived, Todd. Just be grateful for that. Plenty folks don't and plenty folks won't – partly because of our failure here, but don't let that get in the way of your gratitude."

After taking a moment to really digest Bill's response, I turned back to Innsmouth for one last glimpse. "I suppose," I said, taking in the town's ethereal aura and enchanting evil for hopefully the last time, a humbled and fearful respect bestowing itself upon me. "Do you think——?"

"——Oh Jesus Christ, that's enough, Todd. Alright?" Bill's moan held a flavor of sincerity impossible to feign. "Please. Can't we just walk in silence? Grateful silence. It's been a long day, and it's only just gone sunrise, so, yeah… Please. Let's just walk. Let's just walk."

Seeing Bill's long and melancholic gaze (well, in truth, I couldn't particularly tell if it was melancholic or not because of the bloody, fleshy gash in his face where one of his eyes should've been, but I liked to imagine it was), his tired ambling, and – still – his lack of clothes, I decided to simply fulfil his humble wish, and noiselessly walk beside him.

And as we ascended through the shaded forest and crested the hill into relative safety, despite our lack of any real achievements, I felt strangely satisfied. Yes, the warmth of pride lapped gently at my feet as Bill and I headed home from our very first job together.

***

One night, a week or so after making it home, I was lying in bed contemplating what the future held when I was suddenly overcome by the greatest thirst.

Leaving my room to go downstairs and fetch myself a glass of water, I presently found that where the staircase should have been, I was instead standing before the Seventy Steps of Lighter Slumber. In that moment, I realized I was dreaming. A little unnerved, I descended, and soon found myself in that old Cavern of Flame. Nodding to Nasht and Kaman-Thah once again, I passed onto the Seven Hundred Steps of Deeper Slumber with a greater confidence than ever I had had in this world before.

Walking through the Enchanted Woods, the same events occurred as before. A rune beneath my foot, and a magical transportation through the void to that heavenly golden city where I had met Pickman for the second time. In fact, I found myself on the exact same balcony as before, but this time, when I arrived, I found that ghoul Pickman in the middle of a discussion with what looked a witch of sorts.

Her hair was black and deep purple, and her eyes drenched in darkness. Her torn dress was also suitably ravenlike, along with her protracted nails and ink-stained fingers. Looking closely, I noticed that peeking out under her dress, there appeared to be a large set of talons.

"R'lyeh? Are you sure?" Pickman questioned with a tightly trembling growl. The cat with the blazing yellow eyes seemed to be watching the conversation intently from the railing of the balcony.

"Kertuz sarhm," the witch replied in a whispering, vaguely Hispanic intonation.

"Then truly our greatest fears are set to become reality." Turning his head to me, Pickman nodded hello, which in turn alerted the witch to my presence. "Welcome, Todd."

"Hello," I replied.

Turning back to the witch, Pickman added in a low rumble, "Where the moon meets the sun."

Stepping back, she bowed. "O'ohbi llonar zorlehmg." And with that, she faded into the ether like candy floss in water.

Striding towards me with a canine smile, Pickman stretched out his clammy, pale claw of a hand. "Are you well, Todd?"

"I'm confused," I replied as I accepted his bony handshake.

"Close enough. But tell me, has any progress been made as to the finding of your purpose yet? There have been some major developments as of late – I was wondering whether you too were part of this phenomenon?"

"Well," I began before giving him a brief rundown of all I have told you minus a few details such as all the McDonalds and the sorry backrubs. "I mean, I don't know what my purpose was in all that exactly, but… it seems like I'm sort of on the right track. I think. I guess. It sort of felt important."

Pickman had held a quizzical feral eyebrow raised throughout most of my tale, but now that I had finished, I could see he was clearly still stewing over some details that seemed to pain him somewhat. "On a cloud, you say?"

"What? Bill?"

"Yes, you say this 'Bill' rode atop a cloud of sorts?"

"Well, yes."

"Hmm…" He mused this over, clearly rather puzzled, and even seemed to look towards the stoic cat for an answer to his secret question.

"What is it?" I asked.

"Oh, nothing, nothing," he mumbled, dismissing the thing with a wave of his paw. "I'm sure it's nothing." Pickman nodded to himself, deep in thought. "But come with me." He spun on his heels and threw open the French doors beside us before striding into the bedroom. "To have had a direct experience with Dagon is definitely intriguing – I believe it shows you are most certainly on the right path. I wish to make use of the residual mental energy you will have left in your psyche." Approaching a large oil painting of the full moon hanging on the wall, he grabbed ahold of the golden frame and put a foot through the canvas as if it were mere water. Ripples danced away across the lunar surface as Pickman turned back to me and stretched out his claw. "Come on, Todd. Have you ever been to the moon?"

***

Stepping through the painting, I emerged onto the cratered, dusty surface and immediately clasped my mouth, expecting to choke. Pickman laughed as he moved my hand away from my face. "Don't worry, you can breathe here. We're in a dream, remember?" He then turned my attention to a colossal brass bell that hung supportless in the vacuum ahead of us. "I want you to kneel before this bell, and then I shall ring it. Afterwards, I want you to tell me what you saw in its resonance."

As he commanded, I marched forth and knelt before the gargantuan bell which shone brutally in the undiffused light of the burning sun. As Pickman approached the bell I saw moon dust float behind him as if in slow motion, and only then realized that I myself did not seem to be affected by the low gravity of the place.

Holding his arm out, a brass hammer revealed itself beside the bell and gently floated into Pickman's hand as if by its own will. "Close your eyes, dear Todd, and focus on what the bell wishes to show you." I closed my eyes, and seconds later heard the most majestic ringing of a bell I have ever heard – its waves of sound seemed to wash me away from the present moment into fantastical hallucinations and vivid phantasms.

Resplendent visions of the sea rising and swallowing Innsmouth utterly consumed my awareness, and in that moment I saw swarms of those Innsmouth fish devils leading the sea – and those hideous Deep Ones – not only through Innsmouth but through towns and cities all along the east coast; in Salem; New York; Washington; Norfolk; Charleston; Miami; and a thousand other places I did not recognize. It was a total invasion of the land by the sea-dwelling monsters – and yes! Yes, led by a creature of such disturbing and sinister portrayal that I had to expend all mental effort available to me not to open my eyes and be rid of the sight. It was Dagon; that colossal foul serpent with its scales and slimy skin with mottled coral, and its tangled tentacles of numberless description. The creature whose island-sized head we had seen emerging from the sea, and whose echoing scream sent us all into another plane of existence. Yes, that old god of forgotten power was coordinating an attack on the world above from its cyclopean, sprawling, crumbling city that lay deep under the ocean, and had done for aeons. And at its disposal it had not only the legions of Deep Ones, but elephantine beings of formless protoplasm that bubbled in viscous agglutinations. And these immense amorphous beasts were destroying whole streets in their path, and with the rubble, building fortifications of a most strange and wicked architecture. The earth was transforming into a hellscape of deep waters and bright fires, and in that nightmare, I saw no hope. I saw no army holding them back. I saw only futile last stands, and hopeless submissions.

With the fading resonance of the bell, the visions too withered from my sight. Soon, I was left only with darkness. I opened my eyes and told Pickman of all I had saw.

"Fuck," he replied.

***

The next morning, as I served Bill his fried breakfast, I took a chair opposite my friend and prepared myself for what I had promised Pickman I would do.

"What you doing?" Bill asked, adjusting his new leather eyepatch before dipping his hashbrown into a packet of sweet and sour sauce. "Ain't ya got me washing to do?"

"Bill, last night I had another dream… You know, one of *those* dreams."

"What? A sex dream?" Bill asked, a little disgusted and a little confused. "Why you telling me?"

"No, a Dreamland dream. I met Pickman again."

Bill furrowed his brow, displeased. "If you're gonna tell me that old tart said I need to start paying you, then that's just not happening 'cos the financials just aren't there, and I'm giving you room and food and shit which is more than enough and maybe I can give you stock options but—"

"—No, Bill, it's nothing like that," I interrupted.

"Oh, nice. What was it then?" He went to dip his hashbrown again but completely missed the packet, squashing the deep-fried treat against the tabletop. "Still getting used to this one eye thing," he explained.

"Well, it's quite a lot worse than the prospect of paying me for my services, I'm afraid."

"Don't see how it could be but try me."

"There's an invasion coming – orchestrated by Dagon and the Deep Ones. Pickman said he thinks they might be trying to reawaken Cthulhu."

Bill rolled his eye. "No, you're right – that is worse. Fucking Cthulhu. All this notoriety and all he's bloody done is sleep – he doesn't deserve shit. Why does everyone care so much about the bastard? There are way cooler Old Gods out there who would kill for his fame, but do they get so much as a tenth of the respect Cthulhu does? Do they my arse. Makes my bloody blood boil."

"Right, okay," I replied. "But what about the invasion? You know, the invasion of Earth? You care about that, right?"

Bill shrugged. "Easy come, easy go."

"Isn't stopping stuff like this sort of what you're all about? Isn't that sort of the whole reason for your existence? If you don't step up for this then what would have been the point? What would have been the point of all your work? Of your life? It would have been nothing. Your life would've been worthless."

"Jesus, Todd," Bill scoffed. "Bit bloody personal for nine o'clock on a Monday morning, don't ya think? Fuck. That cut deep, Todd. That cut real deep."

"Sorry," I muttered.

Bill put down his knife and fork, and clasped his hands together. "But maybe you're right. Maybe I should do something. Probably. Dunno what, but… Yeah, this is pretty up my alley, you're right."

"Well, Pickman actually asked me if you'd be willing to help – you know, against the invasion. He's sort of putting together a coalition to stop it."

"What?" Bill said, genuinely taken aback and almost blushing. "He wants me?"

"Yeah, he said he thinks you might be able to help, you know, with your knowledge and dream powers and stuff."

"Alright…" Bill tried to suppress his smile and looked back to his food. He shrugged. "Sure. Why not? As long as he don't tell me to do nothing or ask any questions or whatever, then sure." At Bill's acceptance, I couldn't help but smile myself. "Oh, don't do that." Bill moaned.

"What?"

"Smile. You look like a dunce. Go do me washing or something." Assuming he only meant this in jest, I smiled even brighter, ready for his reciprocation. "What the fuck are you doing? I just said don't smile, you twallop." Bill shook his head. "Jesus, you'd think you were one of those special needs kids, some of the stuff you do." He suddenly stopped, mid fork-to-mouth. "Wait, you're not, are you? That would explain quite a lot now, actually, thinking about it."

"No," I confirmed, rather deflated. "Not that I know of."

"Good, alright. It's okay to call you one then."

"Is it?"

Bill shrugged. "I dunno. Got better things to worry about." Bill got back to his breakfast, and I got up from the table, my recruitment mission achieved, ready to leave and start the laundry. "Oh, and before you go," Bill added with a mouth full of sausage. "Cheers for the brekkie, champ – it's a real good one today."

***

Fast-forward to two months later, and here I am, sitting at my desk, finishing this book. It has been a satisfying experience to place my ephemeral memories down in solid ink, and, I believe, it has also gone a long way towards placing some distance in between me and the horrors I have faced – they now seem like merely a fictional story rather than the horrific and disturbing reality I have lived through. So, that's nice.

Pickman hasn't made contact with Bill or I yet, but I feel like soon he must. Every day that goes by without acting is a day less we'll have to prepare for the invasion – but I trust that he has a plan, and that we are merely small cogs in it, so wait we shall.

I do hope this book has been of some interest to you, dear reader, or at the very least, enlightening as to the nightmares that lurk in shadowed streets and oceans deep. And, if you are so inclined, and feel you may be able to help Bill and I in our quest to prevent the rising of the Deep Ones and Dagon's hostile takeover of the land, please do send a fax to +1 666 578-3045 or an email to Bill888888878888@aol.com

Anyhow, I suppose I better end this book – I've got nothing left to say – but I find myself not wanting to. Perhaps because there's a deep dread inside me that when this book is over, when the past is done, then it's onto the future – and I don't think there's a pleasant one awaiting us.

But time marches on. The future's coming whether I want it to or not, and I better get ready for the fight. So, goodbye, my friends. See you on the other side. I hope a few of you join us.

Epilogue.

I know I said I was ending the book in the previous chapter but something incredible has just occurred, and I would be amiss not to include it before I send this manuscript off to print.

I was just cleaning the toilet when I heard the knocker on the door go. "Todd!" Bill cried out from his bedroom as he dried himself off from his bath. Putting down the plunger, I dusted off my clothes and made haste to the front door. Undoing the latch, I swung the thing open and, to my surprise, found no one. I then looked down and, though it was cruel of me, could not help but scream in terror. There was a little girl, of about six years of age – but where her limbs should've been, she had only tentacles, and the skin on her face was a sickly, slimy green.

"Ish my daddy here?" she politely asked.

"Bill!" I screamed. "Bill! Bill!"

Ambling down the stairs, a towel round his waist and a sandwich in hand (with crusts, might I add), Bill called out, "Mormons again?"

"No, No. It's some sort of… creature."

"Jehovah's Witness?"

On reaching the ground floor, and seeing our guest, the sandwich dropped from Bill's hand and made a pleasant splat on the wooden parquet flooring.

"Daddy!" the strange girl called out, holding up a polaroid of a younger Bill with one of her thick, slimy tentacles.

Bill said nothing. Dear Bill just fainted.

Afterword

Did you enjoy that? I hope you did.

Amazon reviews are the single most important factor in improving the lives of independent books. A sentence or two, or even just a rating, would be so very, very appreciated, and it really is quick to do these days.

Every star means an embarrassing amount to me and getting that notification that someone new has just reviewed one of your books really is one of the best feelings as an author – so make that next ding on my phone come from you. If you feel like it.

And while you're at it, make sure to **follow** my Author Profile on Amazon (QR code below). It really helps with the algorithm and also means you'll be the first to find out about any new deals on my other books – and they're pretty good, I think. I mean, they're not terrible.

Read the Next in the Series!

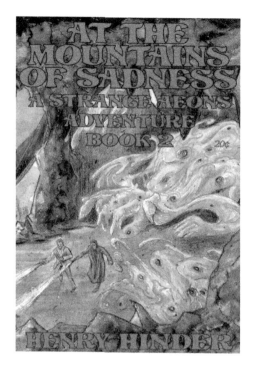

At the Mountains of Sadness
A Strange Aeons Adventure: Book 2

When Bill and Todd are summoned to the remote
Antarctic outpost of Miskatonic University, a place
once inhabited by the enigmatic Elder Things, they
face the mystery left behind by a mad professor
gone rogue.

Available now!

Printed in Great Britain
by Amazon

31973457R00081